DANGER ON THE TRAIL!

Wild Bill had felt this before: this sense that he was both participating in and observing his fate at the same time. It was just like a dream, only he knew this was the real world. And he knew that trouble was coming very soon now, perhaps in the next breath. His fabled guns were less valuable, right now, than his honed reflexes and quick reactions. But he mustn't miss the slightest clue.

Such as those few small pebbles just now trickling down the slope to his right. True, the movement was so slight a bird or scurrying insect might have caused it.

"Freeze, kid," he called back. "Hug the slope."

Immediately Josh reined in his piebald. Fire-away was trained to stop immediately whenever his reins touched the ground. Wild Bill tossed them forward, then drew his right-side Colt and stared straight overhead.

The solid mass of the slope gave way to deep indigo sky. Stars glowed like scattered crystals. But Bill's narrowed eyes detected a place where the dense pattern of stars seemed to be blotted out. As if by some object. It was right where the sky met the top of the slope.

And whatever that object was, it seemed to be moving.

This time, Bill didn't bother to hold his voice down.

"Kid, this is it! Wheel and retreat! Rockslide!"

The *Wild Bill* series:
#1: **DEAD MAN'S HAND**
#2: **THE KINKAID COUNTY WAR**
#3: **BLEEDING KANSAS**

WILD BILL
YUMA BUSTOUT

JUDD COLE

LEISURE BOOKS NEW YORK CITY

A LEISURE BOOK®

January 2000

Published by

Dorchester Publishing Co., Inc.
276 Fifth Avenue
New York, NY 10001

If you purchased this book without a cover you should be aware that this book is stolen property. It was reported as "unsold and destroyed" to the publisher and neither the author nor the publisher has received any payment for this "stripped book."

Copyright © 2000 by Dorchester Publishing Co., Inc.

All rights reserved. No part of this book may be reproduced or transmitted in any form or by any electronic or mechanical means, including photocopying, recording or by any information storage and retrieval system, without the written permission of the Publisher, except where permitted by law.

ISBN 0-8439-4674-1

The name "Leisure Books" and the stylized "L" with design are trademarks of Dorchester Publishing Co., Inc.

Printed in the United States of America.

YUMA BUSTOUT

Chapter One

"Don't I *wish* that killing Hickok could be our first play? Lorenzo, I'd give my share of the swag for the pleasure of sending him under. Hadn't been for Hickok, us two'd be living like kings right now. But planting that pretty son of a bitch will just have to wait a bit."

Fargo Danford fell silent, his murky, mud-colored eyes watching the nearest guard. Sweat poured out of the greasy tangle of Danford's hair. But the blazing desert sun and air evaporated it almost immediately.

"Christ, I can't even spit," complained Lorenzo Hanchon. "Lookit that bastard McQuady, boss—rubbing it in."

A big, soft-bellied guard, one of four men assigned to watch this work detail, deliberately made a big show of enjoying a cool drink of water.

Holding his sawed-off shotgun prominently in one

hand, McQuady used the other to raise a goatskin water bag to his lips. Not the foul, alkali-tainted water rationed out to inmates, either. This was clean, cool, deep-table water from a spring well beyond the nearby Colorado River.

All twenty of the inmates watched in bitter envy as McQuady spat out the first mouthful. Then he drank deeply, letting water run off his chin into the burning sand.

"A *free* man," he called out, taunting the prisoners, "can have him a cool drink any damn time he fancies. *You* stupid birds, however, belong to me now! My little slaves!"

Danford watched him with an emotionless face, dusty and beard-smudged. Those murky eyes narrowed with homicidal hatred. Of the guards who were about to die hard deaths here today, Danford figured this pig McQuady deserved the hardest.

Danford grabbed hold of an eighty-pound rock from the man behind him. Grunting through clenched teeth, he passed it on to Lorenzo. They had been assigned to shore up one of the massive stone bulwarks supporting the Territorial Prison at Yuma.

All around them, as far as the eye could see, the arid brown folds of the Yuma Desert stretched on unbroken, ending in a shimmering heat haze on the far horizon. The summer air felt brittle with warmth that seemed to radiate from a giant furnace.

Lorenzo's kid brother, Willard, worked in the group nearest to Danford and Lorenzo. In that second group was also the fourth surviving member of Danford's gang, a taciturn half-breed named Coyote.

Willard, quickly checking the whereabouts of the

Yuma Bustout

guards, took a chance and edged closer to his brother and Fargo Danford. Like those of many of his fellow convicts, Willard's feet were wrapped in burlap and his pants were out at the knees. The glaring sunlight showed beggar-lice leaping from many scalps.

"You sure they'll be there?" Willard demanded in a low tone.

Danford gave a curt nod. "Damn, you're gettin' worse than your brother, playin' the female. Settle down—I already said they'll be there."

Danford glanced farther up the steep stone slope. A flat slab of black shale lay maybe ten yards above them now.

He was indeed confident that four good-quality killing knives were hidden under that stone. Most of these prison guards were nothing but criminals themselves. They all knew that the Danford gang had robbed a bullion coach carrying silver bars bound for the U.S. Mint at Denver. Although Wild Bill Hickok eventually killed three of them and collared the rest, the silver had never been recovered. It was rumored to be buried somewhere in Mexico, most likely northern Sonora State.

So Danford had struck a "gentleman's agreement" with one of the greedier guards, who had licked his boots here at Yuma. Four good knives for one thirty-pound bar of silver, payable in the near future if escape succeeded.

Willard returned to his work gang, but not before McQuady saw Danford talking to him. McQuady's long whip cracked like green wood snapping, and fire sliced deep into Danford's burly back.

"Get back to work, cockroach, or I'll step on you

Judd Cole

even harder!" McQuady roared. He'd turned doubly mean from the day that Danford refused to strike terms with him.

"There'll be no lolly-gaggers on my watch!" he added importantly, proud he was sergeant of the guard.

Even before the fiery pain in his back subsided, a faint shadow of smile touched Danford's lips.

"McQuady is all mine," he told Lorenzo through clenched teeth.

Coyote, who had the sharp hearing of his namesake, heard this. He looked over at his boss and flashed his lipless grin.

Fargo Danford was the natural leader in any group of hard, immoral men—the one man who could always concentrate their efforts toward evil. But even he shuddered inwardly at the nameless depravity in Coyote's flat eyes. When those eyes looked at any man for more than a few seconds, they were generally measuring him for a grave.

For the laborers, the morning advanced with torturous slowness. The workers tried to hug a narrowing ring of shade around the base of Prison Hill. Prisoners at Yuma were not issued headgear because the open desert could not be crossed without hats. One more reason, among several good ones, why very few men ever attempted to escape from Yuma.

Piles of bleached bones marked the open graves of the few who had tried. The relentless and unforgiving desert was considered the most effective guard of all.

At midday the men were allowed to rest briefly, each receiving a dipper of foul water and a hard biscuit. When the break was over, Danford's group was sent higher up the rock-strewn slope.

Yuma Bustout

Lorenzo deliberately blocked the view of his leader while Danford quickly slid the shale aside.

"Struck a lode!" he whispered joyously.

Four simple but well-balanced metal knives lay under the stone. Dags, Danford noted with satisfaction—compact but deadly, with curved hilts to keep the killing hand from sliding forward. And sharp, narrow blades meant to reach and puncture internal organs, sever major arteries.

He hastily flipped one back to Lorenzo and put the others inside his shirt.

"McQuady is mine," he repeated in a voice that reached his gang but not the guards.

Once again heaving stones into place, Danford added, "Willard, I'll give you and Coyote your blades real soon now. Lorenzo? You're going to take Hobson down. Willard will do Mosley. Coyote kills Whittier."

Danford's bloodshot eyes cut to McQuady before he added, "Wait for my command, boys. And don't forget. After you sink the blade in deep, give it what they call the Spanish twist."

"Kid," said J. B. Hickok as he and newspaperman Joshua Robinson emerged from the red-granite courthouse on Denver's bustling Silver Street, "didn't I warn you months ago that the Wild West is more boring than wild? We brought that jasper in without a whimper. Hell, he even asked for my autograph. Used to be, they'd cuss me a little."

"They sure cussed you up in Kinkaid County, Wyoming," Josh reminded him. "Shot at you plenty, too. And how 'bout that sniper mess you cleaned up in Abilene?"

Bill paused on the wide steps and slid a thin Mexican cigar from his vest. He glanced into the sky. "Past three, by the sun."

Then Bill looked at Josh and finally replied, "The thing of it is, I don't think about the roughest scrapes." Bill tried to keep a match lit in the wind. "I mean, you look at it logically, and hell, I'm already dead."

Bill gave up the idea of smoking in that wind. He sent a careful glance all around them. Then he led Josh down to the newly paved sidewalk. Bill preferred boards, for they sent warnings to an observant man.

"I'm in a good mood," Wild Bill confided. "So don't spoil it. Pinkerton's got nothing but routine jobs lined up for us. A water-rights battle up in Weld County, some two-bit rustler camp in western Kansas. Piddling stuff, just like I requested."

Most of the time while he spoke, Bill kept his head tilted forward, taking advantage of the shadow cast by his broad-brimmed black hat. Somewhat fastidious about his appearance, Hickok wore a long duster to protect his suit. It also covered a heavy shell belt and a pair of ivory-grip Colt Peacemakers.

"I know you and your beloved *New York Herald* thrive on derring-do," Bill went on, heading west toward the huge Emporium and Denver's new hotel district. "But I've got my belly full of 'terrific sensations.' Right now all I want are clean sheets, a bottle of Old Taylor, a dark bar, and a fair woman."

Wild Bill steered Josh through a shouting confusion of vendors at the corner, then onto Copper Street.

"Pinkerton," he said with a satisfied grin, "doesn't even expect us until day after tomorrow. Even better, he doesn't have any idea in hell that I usually take a room at the Crystal Palace when I'm in Denver. That's two whole days to relax, play poker, and eat like by-God white men."

Bill's good mood drove him to slap Josh heartily between his narrow shoulders, almost making the youth stumble.

"Who knows, Longfellow? Quite a few new saloons in town. Maybe you'll be able to impress a hurdy-gurdy gal with that paper collar and your store-bought vocabulary. Some of 'em climb all over a bookish chap."

"I ain't bookish," Josh protested. "Just smart."

They were sheltered from the wind now by the high buildings. Bill poked the cigar between his teeth again and produced a match.

He was about to light it with his thumbnail when, abruptly, a pistol shot startled everyone in the street.

Josh gaped when the match flared to life without Bill's help.

"God kiss me!" Hickok almost moaned the words, for he realized immediately who fired the bullet that just missed his face by inches.

"Bill Hickok, you purty specimen of man-flesh!" roared a drunk, disheveled, stout, and homely young woman wearing an immaculate Stetson. "God dawg, but you're tonic to a horny gal's eyes!"

"Jane's found us again," Josh said. "And she's drunk as a monkey."

"The way you say," Bill agreed. His gunmetal eyes were already searching for an escape alley. "And she's planted herself square in front of the Crystal Palace. She's a damned curse, but that woman is sharper than a Navajo tracker."

Jane finished another bottle of "medicinal" Doyle's

Hop Bitters, the popular curative she supposedly sold from her buckboard wagon. In fact, she consumed three bottles for every one she retailed.

"Bill!" she yelled in a voice like gravel rattling in a sluice gate. "The hell you doin', hangin' round with all these soft-handed town bastards? Honey, let's scalp a few of these perfumed clerks!"

But Denver was not the wide-open, anything-goes town it had once been. Jane's illegal gunfire had alerted the city roundsmen. Even now, Josh saw several constables with a lockup wagon round the corner behind Calamity Jane.

"C'mon, kid," Bill said, ducking into a service alley that led to the rear of the hotel. "They'll arrest her, all right, but it'll get ugly. As for me . . ."

Bill grinned again, his good mood undaunted by this brief sighting of his chief female nemesis.

"I meant what I said. We got two whole days before Pinkerton gives us our next set of marching orders. Jane'll be locked up at least seventy-two hours. Ain't nobody or nothing on God's green earth going to spoil our big time."

Chapter Two

During the long afternoon work shift, Fargo Danford managed to sneak knives to Willard Hanchon and Coyote without being spotted. Now the gang had only to wait for the best opportunity.

It came near the end of the grueling work shift. By then McQuady and the other three guards were tired and bored, their senses dulled by the unrelenting sun and heat. Too, they were distracted by thoughts of hot food and soft beds.

"Lissenup, birds!" McQuady barked. "Muster for roll call! Time to stick you roaches back in your holes!"

The guards, Danford realized triumphantly, had made the fatal mistake of clustering up close together, sharing some jokes. He sent the high sign to his men, then waited until each had lined up with his assigned target.

Danford gave one curt nod, and all four struck like adders.

It took no more than three seconds to close the gap. McQuady didn't even get his scattergun up before Danford's blade plunged between his fourth and fifth ribs, straight into the heart.

"I just cut you to trap bait, big man," Danford taunted the guard in his last living moment. "Now go burn in hell!"

McQuady's knees folded like empty cloth, and he fell in a lifeless heap, heels scratching the desert sand a few times.

The rest of the convicts were too stunned to react.

McQuady and his men disarmed the dead men, taking their Colt side arms and stiff-flap holsters as well as their shotguns and spare shells. Each man also took any clothes and boots that fit.

"Stay close to the hill," Danford warned his men. "You leave the shadow, they can spot you from the wall. Gradual on that," he added, grabbing the water away from Lorenzo. "We'll be needing it."

Danford looked at the other prisoners. "Rest of you, do what you want to! I got no dicker with any of you. But nobody goes with us!"

"No offense, Fargo," said a big redhead named Slappy Grabowitz. "But nobody *wants* to go."

"Hell, Fargo," said another voice. "That desert is just hell turned inside out. Nobody's whipped it yet. Leastways, not without horses or mules."

Danford said nothing to that. It was gospel truth, but his gang would soon have horses, too. That was part of the deal he had made.

About thirty very hard miles from there, a remote

Yuma Bustout

way station served the Tucson-Yuma stage line. Only a weekly mail coach made the desolate run, occasionally bringing a passenger or two. Four good saddle mounts and a pack animal should be waiting for Danford's gang in a shaded *barranca* near the station.

"Let's move out," Danford told his men. All four were also wearing the guards' hats. "They'll likely spot us while we're still in rifle range, so don't move in a straight line and make aiming easy for them. Run like your ass is on fire until you're outta range. Coyote! The hell you doing?"

Coyote said nothing, only flashing his lipless grin. He squatted beside McQuady and tore the dead man's trousers open.

"I promised this son of a bitch something," Coyote finally replied.

"Hell!"

Danford averted his eyes while the half-breed castrated the corpse.

Coyote stood up, wiping his knife off on his trousers. "That's for the trackers coming after us," he explained in his flat, toneless voice. "Gives 'em a little incentive not to hurry."

A young Army officer in a dusty tunic opened the stagecoach door and swung down the step.

"Welcome to Joshua Tree Station, ladies," the escort said smartly. "Last stop in the Yuma Desert. There's food and drink ready inside. We'll be in Yuma before nightfall. Watch your step, ladies."

The first woman he handed down was Anne Jacobs, wife of Arizona's territorial governor, John C. Jacobs. Anne was a stately, mature beauty of thirty-five, still quite striking and slim-waisted. Obviously, though, she was tired and heat-wilted from the arduous trip.

The second woman to step down was Anne's even more famous sister, Constance Emmerick, fourteen years younger and still unmarried. She wore a straw hat trimmed with a blue ribbon and an ostrich feather.

"My stars!" she exclaimed, looking at the low adobe-brick station with its crude brick *horno* out front for baking. "I hoped there might be plumbing arrangements here, Lieutenant!"

"Uhh—sorry, ma'am. Very few city-style amenities, I'm afraid."

He nodded apologetically toward a rickety jakes behind the station.

"We don't usually get Shakesperean actresses on this route. If you—ahh—visit the facilities, ma'am, be careful of scorpions and such. I'll run in first and scare off any snakes."

Connie paled noticeably. That made her bold dark eyes look even bolder. "Scare off any— Is there plumbing in Yuma?"

The officer wasn't sure exactly what Constance meant by "plumbing," but he was too embarrassed to ask.

"Not so's you'd notice, ma'am. But there's fewer scorpions and snakes there."

"Then I believe I'll wait, thank you."

Anne smiled at her timid sister while the officer hustled on ahead to open the door for them. Both women moved a bit stiffly toward the station. Their bodies were aching and sore from the jolting coach. Even leather thoroughbraces hardly smoothed the rugged old Federal Road, once known as the Gila River Trace.

"I know this must all seem quite a shock after Boston," Anne comforted the younger woman. "I realized that when I went back this time, honey. This is all so primitive and rude, isn't it? But I can assure you, dear, Jim Paxton's ranch is the most civilized place in this territory. Indoor plumbing, an icehouse, even a hydro spa."

Connie took heart. "You know, Jim told me he's even added a small theater off the library wing so we can present dramas. I won't have to give up my acting!"

"Give it up! Nonsense, Jim swears he'll do nothing to hide such a light as yours! And do you know? The black-marble fireplace mantels were all imported from Italy!"

Anne nattered on, trying to reassure her worried sister. Connie Emmerick's stunning interpretations of Juliet and Desdemona and Lady Macbeth had earned her international acclaim. But like her older sister, she was an ambitious woman who respected Commerce as well as Art. She had to, for she required a vast fortune to fulfill her aesthetic goals.

Thus, she had come to remote Arizona in what amounted to an arranged marriage. Arizona cattle baron Jim Paxton was Governor Jacobs's best friend and rumored to be the wealthiest man between the Rio and the Tetons. He was also an adoring follower of Connie's art, having seen her act in several acclaimed productions.

The two women paused at the open door of the hovel. A bright *ristra*, a string of dried red peppers, hung beside the door. Flat corn tortillas baked in the *horno* nearby. Somebody within was complaining in rapid Spanish.

"I like new things," Connie admitted. "But by degrees! This is all so foreign and queer. I feel as if we've ended up on the moon by mistake."

She glanced to her right just in time to watch a yellow-gray coyote slink off through a dry wash, grinning at some sly secret she didn't know.

Despite the wilting heat, the young actress's cheeks still glowed like Roman Beauties.

"It's all so . . . still and boring," Connie added. "I suppose those nature lovers and that crowd enjoy it. But it lacks any culture or . . . excitement."

"Boring? Careful," Anne warned her. "We who live here prefer to call it the 'sleepy Southwest.' But don't be deceived by first impressions, dear. Sometimes it can be far more exciting than one might wish."

Connie cast one last, despairing glance around the desolate landscape. The only sound, in that moment, was the dusty twang of grasshoppers. At least, she supposed they were grasshoppers. God only knew, out here.

"If you say so, big sister," she said doubtfully. "But so far, I don't feel much like a bride. More like a little girl who wants to go back home."

The four of them pressed on toward the east with a grim sense of purpose, knowing trackers would not be far behind them.

Their stolen hats protected their skulls. But treacherous desert dust devils pelted them with maddening frequency, driving irritating sand under their eyelids and swelling them shut.

Yuma Bustout

" 'Em damn horses better be there," Lorenzo Hanchon kept repeating.

"Look, they'll be there," Danford assured him confidently. "You bawl too damn much."

"Bawl, my ass! We'll never clear this desert withouten we got horses."

"All your damn female talk," Coyote said in his eerie monotone, "won't make horses be where they ain't."

Lorenzo scowled but said nothing to this. He and his brother Willard wouldn't admit it to Danford, but both of them feared and disliked Coyote. He was a strange one who spent so much time alone he didn't think like other men—nor act like them. Trouble was, Danford clearly favored Coyote.

"Don't matter nohow," Danford announced triumphantly. "Look out past that low mesa, gents! There's our horses!"

"Hot damn!" Willard tossed a handful of sand at his brother. "Satisfied now, calamity howler?"

"Just hold on," Danford said when he and his men reached the edge of the jagged ravine where the horses stood grazing.

From here, Joshua Tree Station was clearly visible about a hundred yards farther on. Danford pointed at the waiting coach. The driver was busy unhitching the team so they could drink from a stone trough around to one side of the low building.

"Now, see, I didn't expect no coach," Danford said slowly, thinking more than conversing.

"So what?" Lorenzo retorted. He was already busy getting first pick of the horses. "It's a way station, ain't it?"

"That's just a mail sack up topside," Willard added. "From the mail-sorting deal they got at Fort Huachuca. We ain't made nothing from stealing mail, remember? You open a hunnert envelopes for maybe ten dollars cash money, it's—"

"I ain't interested in the mail, you stupid fool." Danford nodded as a young officer stepped outside of the building to tend to his own horse. "That means it's carrying something besides mail. He ain't in transit—he's an escort."

Lorenzo frowned, still not impressed. "What I say, we just grab leather and hightail it into Old Mex."

"Slow down! We'll dust hocks for Mex, all right," Danford assured him. "But first we check out that coach."

"We got what we need!" Lorenzo protested. "This ain't none of our funerals."

"It'll be yours," Danford assured him, "you don't quit talking against me all the time. Coyote!"

"Yo!"

"You and Willard ain't no whiners! You two close in behind that line of sand dunes over there. Me 'n' Lorenzo the Mouth will come up the other way behind that line of palo duro."

Danford broke open his scattergun and checked the chambers.

"Coyote and Willie, you two get a tight bead on that driver. When you hear me plug the soldier, you do the same for the driver. Then hustle your butts 'round back and cover the door. We don't know who's inside."

The approach went off without a hitch. By the time Danford stepped out from behind the line of scrawny palo duro trees, he was within thirty feet of the soldier, .44 at the ready.

The officer had just loosed the bridle and dropped the bit on his big cavalry sorrel. He was leading it toward the corner of the adobe station when he abruptly spotted two scruffy, hard-looking men out of the corner of his eye.

Danford fired twice before the young soldier even cleared his holster. The first bullet only chipped his collarbone. But the second caught him dead center and slammed him against the hovel. A second later, Coyote's shotgun roared and the driver's face melted in a hurtling wall of buckshot.

Lorenzo was indeed a complainer, but he always did his share of the dangerous work. A woman inside screamed when he came bustling through the front door, side arm blazing to clear a hole.

"It's all clear!" he shouted a moment later to the rest outside. "Willard, you son of a bitch!" he added. "I want shares on that loot!"

True, even then Willard was going through the dead driver's pockets. But Fargo Danford had found something much more interesting inside.

Two fine-looking, well-dressed women huddled together at one end of a long plank table. A stooped old Mexican woman, wearing a dark rebozo around her head, still stood beside the table, clay water jar in hand. An old man, probably her husband, stood near a smoking pot on the stove, ladle in hand.

"Well goddamn well," Danford said slowly, still studying the two Anglo women. This was woman-scarce country. *And these two* . . . he thought. *Lookit all that velvet*. And what it hid was no doubt velvet, too.

"Ain't you two something?" he said in a low, husky voice. But it was loud and mean again when he added: "*Señora!* Knock up some grub, pronto! *Comida,* you savvy!"

"*Sí, senor. Momentito.*"

Willard came stomping in, Coyote right behind him.

"Well, kiss my ass!" Willard exclaimed, seeing the women. "I want shares, too!"

"Gentlemen," Anne Jacobs said bravely, "we are both expected soon in Yuma by two very powerful men. I am not making threats, only warning you. Any harm to us will cost you dearly."

Coyote gave a quick, sharp bark of laughter at this.

"She's a high-toned bitch, ain't she?" Lorenzo said. "But I like the younger one. Think I'll top 'em both, make one watch the other get it."

"*Don't* touch me!" Connie protested, shying back from Coyote's probing hand.

"Brash as a rented mule, ain't she?" Lorenzo said. A second later, both women gasped in shock when Lorenzo slapped Connie hard enough to make her eyes water.

Coyote giggled like a child in school.

"Both you bitches," Lorenzo said, "your tongues're swinging way too loose. Got it? Best tighten 'em up 'fore I cut 'em out and cure 'em."

"Just hold your water, boys," Danford cut in.

He stared hard at the younger woman. "I'll be hog-tied and earmarked if I ain't seen that little gal's pretty face somewheres. What's your name, cupcake?"

One corner of Connie's lower lip was already swollen. "Miss Constance Emmerick," she replied with some difficulty. "Of Boston."

"Well, kiss my ass!" Willard stared at his leader.

Yuma Bustout

"It's 'at actress, boss! Jim Paxton's mail-order whore. I've heard the prison screws talking about it."

Danford nodded. His eyes shifted to the older woman.

"If these two lookers ain't sisters," he said, "I'll eat this flap hat. Which means thissen must be Anne Jacobs, am I right, sugar?"

"The governor's woman?" Willard said, and Coyote began laughing so hard he had to sit down.

"That's right," Danford said. "No more hitting them, boys. Them ain't faces to mess up."

He looked at the Mexicans. "Snap it up with that grub, ah? *De prisa*, damnit!"

Danford turned to Coyote. "Climb up on the coach and keep watch. I'll run you out some grub when it's ready. We got to clear out 'fore them trackers get here."

"What about them?" Lorenzo demanded, staring at the frightened sisters. "We at least gonna take 'em out back and have a little fun before we leave?"

Danford shook his head. "You see here, that's why I run this gang. On account you're so damn thick-skull stupid, Lorenzo. We're taking our *fun* with us. You think John Jacobs and Jim Paxton will risk their women's lives lightly—or cheap? Boys, them two bitches are the keys to the mint! They're going with us."

Chapter Three

As events worked out, Wild Bill's two-day "big time" in Denver was abruptly lopped in half—and it was the best half that Bill lost.

Hickok's first priority wasn't a woman but a good poker game. Josh trailed him from saloon to saloon, dealing the hands and enjoying the free lunch set out to entice drinkers.

Wild Bill was kind to the sporting girls. But as always, he paid no serious attention to gals plying carnal wares. Josh knew he had more refined tastes in women.

And toward the end of that first day, Bill met a lass more to his liking.

Her name was Marie Marchand, a singer at the Silver Street Music Hall. Bill sent Josh packing while he and Miss Marchand enjoyed a good dinner and a play.

Josh returned to the hotel early in the evening and stopped by Bill's room. He could tell from Hickok's little self-satisfied smile that he had another rendezvous planned later with the French singer.

The suite included a fancy velvet bellpull for summoning porters. Bill tugged on it, and scant moments later a boy in pompous hotel livery appeared in the doorway.

"Give these a coat of polish, wouldja, fellow?" Bill said, handing the kid his boots and a fifty-cent piece.

"You bet, Wild Bill! But you can keep the money if I could have a bullet instead?"

Bill grinned at the youth's eager foolishness. His shell belt hung from one of the bed posts. Bill thumbed a cartridge out and gave it to the porter. A round from his belt was considered the best talisman on the frontier.

Bill was in a good mood, and Josh saw one reason why—there were already two empty Old Taylor bottles on the highboy, and Bill was working through number three.

Wild Bill saw Josh eyeing the bottles.

"Kid, no need to frown like Carrie Nation. When it comes to drinking good whiskey, it's better to pass out hard than to hedge. I got two whole entire goddamn undivided days that Al Pinkerton can't ruin for me, damn his slave-driving bones back to Dundee anyway! And Calamity Jane is locked down tight. Son, Bill Hickok has gone to the only heaven he knows."

Bill fell silent while he topped off his glass. A sash window overlooking the street was wide open. Both men heard it simultaneously, the distinctive patter of a newsboy below:

Yuma Bustout

"Exter! Exter! Read all about it! Ter-*iff*-ic sensation! Danford gang escapes from Yuma, kidnaps actress Connie Emmerick! Read all about it, folks, ter-*iff*-ic sensation!"

"Jees!" Josh stared hard at Bill, who stood frozen with his glass halfway to his lips. "The Danford gang, Bill! Man alive, you sent them to prison."

Hickok slowly set his glass down without drinking.

"The Danford gang," he said almost reverently. "Now, there's a sweet outfit. I woulda killed every one of those chuckleheads, saved the people of Arizona Territory the cost of feeding the murdering scuts."

"So why didn't you?"

"They didn't know my gun was empty when I jumped them, that's why. Marched 'em forty miles to jail with an empty shooter."

The memory made Hickok smile, strong white teeth flashing under his neat mustache. But the smile disappeared in an instant.

"Anyhow," he told Josh, "it ain't our picnic now, kid."

"Sure," Josh agreed. "Somebody else's headache."

Three urgent raps on the door suddenly hinted otherwise.

"Jamie! Jamie lad, are you in there?"

Bill recognized Allan Pinkerton's sonorous brogue and began quietly cursing while Josh let the man in.

"How'd *you* know about this place?" Hickok demanded by way of greeting.

Pinkerton was middle-aged, carried a prosperous paunch, and wore one of the new two-piece suits of the professional class.

"Jamie, this is my city. I'm a detective, after all."

"You're a damned piker! I want more money. And

more time off, damnit! Kid, tell him all about the riots back east to get this new ten-hour workday."

Pinkerton assumed the face of a wooden Indian, as he always did at requests for money.

"Dinna fash yourself, lad. I'll talk to my accountant."

Bill scowled and polished off the bourbon in his glass. "You said that last time. Allan, I have needs."

Josh watched Pinkerton cast an ironic glance around the plush suite. A bottle of champagne protruded from a wicker bucket filled with ice. Empty Old Taylor bottles dotted the place. Bill's new forty-dollar evening jacket was draped over a chair. And earlier, a hopeful lass at the music hall had tossed a pair of frilly "step-ins" to Bill. Pinkerton stared at the lacy garment, which Bill had tucked into his right holster.

"I see that you have needs, Jamie," Pinkerton finally replied. "You're a top hand, Hickok, but this high life will soften you. You were quite spartan when I knew you during the war. Lived off the land, all that."

Bill stared at his boss's paunch and soft white hands.

"You and the kid here, Allan, couple of temperance ladies. Never mind that hogwash. It's this Danford business brought you here, am I right?"

"Yes, and—"

"Forget it," Bill said, shaking his head violently. "I've already skinned that grizz. Somebody else's turn."

"Yes, but—"

"No," Bill said again. "Forget it. You gave me your word, Allan—just some workaday cases for a while, tracking down rustler camps and such."

"I know that, Jamie, but—"

"Stick your 'buts' back in your pocket! That's the jurisdiction of U.S. marshals," Bill insisted. "Or the Army out of Fort Huachuca. Not private ops."

"The normal jurisdiction has been rescinded by order of Governor Jacobs." Pinkerton had finally succeeded at shoehorning a complete sentence between Bill's objections.

Now it was Josh who spoke up.

"Why?" he demanded, beating Hickok to it. The reporter had learned that Bill's misery was a journalist's windfall.

"Because," the Scotsman replied, "he doesn't trust them. He only trusts the man who collared the Danford gang once before. John Jacobs dotes on his wife, and she deserves his devotion. I've met Anne Jacobs. She's a credit to womanhood."

"I'm sure she's a saint," Bill replied sarcastically. "Allan, I've got plans for tonight—*all* night, if you take my drift? Plans for tomorrow, too."

Pinkerton, however, was a crafty handler of men. Now he looked over at Josh. But his words were intended for Hickok's ears.

"Tragedy, really. *Two* fine women in terrible jeopardy. Constance Emmerick may be the best female Shakespearean thespian currently treading the boards."

"She *is* the best," Bill chimed in reluctantly. "A real bitch offstage, though. I saw her perform at the National Theater in San Francisco. I took roses to her dressing room."

"What happened?" Josh demanded.

Bill scowled at him. "I guess somebody put them in water. I wouldn't know—she had some big brick outhouse named Olaf deposit me on my face in the alley out back."

"She's an *artiste*," Pinkerton coaxed, knowing that intrigued Bill. "Being bitches is what they do. Besides, I hear she's *nice* to men who bore her. Sounds like you might have interested her, Jamie."

Josh watched Bill's scowl become a thoughtful frown as he considered this possibility. In fact, Josh knew Bill would accept the case. He seldom refused a job. Like many men out west, Bill lived for today and never saved for "retirement." Bill belonged to that vast class of men who either worked or died.

"You know they'll escape into Mexico," Bill said. "Their stolen silver's hidden down there somewhere."

Pinkerton tried not to gloat as he realized he'd hooked his fish.

"They will," he agreed. "That's another reason why Governor Jacobs can't rely on U.S. authorities. An *official* pursuit into Mexico requires a signed letter of marque to waive international law. But the political situation between us and Mexico is at low ebb these days. It'd take time and money to bribe it through their bureaucracy."

Bill nodded. "Wouldn't matter much anyway. Signed papers from Mexico City don't cut much ice with the northern provinces. It's snake eat snake in Mexico. Best to fight shy of everybody, papers or no."

Bill's eyes cut to Josh. "There's a hoodoo on me, Longfellow. Must be Jane's curse."

"There's a private train waiting for you right now," Pinkerton said. "It'll take you to Gila Bend. You'll have to ride in from there."

"Best get over to Thompson's livery," Bill told Josh, "and pick up our horses and rigging. Take them to the freight siding. And wipe that grin off your pan, kid. You ain't locked horns yet with the Danford gang. We got some more dirt to shovel. Some *deep* dirt."

Even as Wild Bill boarded his private train in Denver, two worried men met seven hundred miles away at Jim Paxton's ranch north of Yuma.

"Any more word from Pinkerton yet?" Paxton asked.

"Not yet," Governor Jacobs replied. "But he assured me he'd talk to Hickok immediately and then wire me back."

John Jacobs was short and stout, with a big, square, solid jaw that matched his tenacious business sense. But right now there were big pouches like bruises under his eyes. He was gnawing himself inside over his decision to let his wife and sister-in-law travel the notorious Old Federal Road.

"When I requested a military escort," Jacobs said yet again, "I expected at least four seasoned troopers. Not just one shavetail lieutenant fresh from West Point! Besides, how could I figure on a prison break?"

"All that is smoke behind us now," Paxton reminded him. "The point now is the time we're wasting while we wait for Hickok to surface in some Denver whorehouse. Anne and Connie's chances decrease with every hour we waste."

Paxton, like his shorter and stouter friend, was around forty. Some men mellow with age and prosperity, as Jacobs himself had done; others, like Paxton, get hardened and narrowed. He was a man of strong feelings, but also a muddy thinker.

"The *point*," Jacobs corrected him, "is to do the best we can to get our women back alive."

"Alive . . . and untouched. I'm damned if I'll marry any woman the Danford gang has sullied."

The two men were alone in the main parlor of Paxton's ranch house, a sumptuous room featuring varnished oil paintings in gold scrollwork frames and red plush furniture with fancy knotted fringe.

"Purity doesn't amount to a hill of beans," Jacobs retorted, "in a dead fiancée."

Thus reined in by logic, Paxton returned to the subject of Wild Bill Hickok.

"The man's an arrogant, self-indulgent peacock! His people back in Illinois are as common as your uncle Bill. Yet Hickok swaggers it up big. He can't stick to his own class of women. Always bedding some foreign princess or . . . actress. And these fawning magpies in the press egg it on."

"His personality be damned," Jacobs told his friend. "Hickok's good at what he does. The best. That's all I care about. You worry too damn much about his 'temporary marriages.'"

"Easy for you to say, John. You're safe from his tomcatting. Anne's comely, all right, but Hickok will fix his fancy on Connie. And mister, mark my words—Jim Paxton doesn't take *any* man's leavings, least of all a puffed-up swell like Hickok."

Jacobs shook his head in frustration. "Our women could be dead right now, and all you can harp about is Hickok putting horns on you. You've got your priorities hindside foremost, Jim."

"I do want Connie back safe," Paxton insisted. "If Hickok can do it, fine and dandy. I can't abide the man, but I'll gladly match whatever you pay him. But sending Bill Hickok to protect beautiful women is like sending a fox to guard the henhouse."

"Better the fox than the butcher," Jacobs said. "And Fargo Danford's gang is *four* butchers."

Chapter Four

La Cola was a tiny, dusty, desert-flats pueblo located ninety miles south of the U.S.-Mexico border in Sonora.

Its name, Fargo Danford assured his men from his stubbled deadpan, was local slang for the ass end of the world. La Cola possessed only alkali water, one road that was more like a goat trail, and no reason whatsoever for going there except to end your life.

Long ago the place might have dried up in the desert winds, but for one reason—various Spanish and Mexican generals found it valuable as a far-north staging area. A rear base for troops and supplies during campaigns against the Tejanos, the gringos, or thieving *indios* like the Apaches and Comanches.

But nowadays it had become an outlaw haven for men on the dodge along the vast, desolate stretch of borderland. It belonged to no nation, was in fact a third nation, La Frontera, with its own laws and its own crimes, its own harsh code of survival.

But La Cola also had the Danford gang's hidden silver *barras*. Twenty of them, thirty pounds each—six hundred pounds of the purest, finest silver from the mines near Vera Cruz. They would fetch $40,000 American, cash money over the counter and no questions asked. Ten thousand dollars for each member of the gang, at a time when most men survived on less than $400 a year.

Several times Danford reminded his men of these key facts. So the escapees moved steadily southeast from the Yuma Desert, showing good discipline and letting brisk desert wind and shifting sands obliterate their sign.

Danford had decided to take a direct route to La Cola rather than waste time and effort laying down false trails. Well-armed soldiers were safe, but few men were fool enough to enter La Cola. Danford himself dreaded the idea. Since the silver was not in town, but nearby, he meant to avoid the pueblo.

Their prisoners were increasingly miserable and frightened, but Danford refused to let the women's suffering slow his group. At least there were enough horses. The gang added the dead officer's well-trained sorrel to their string. And the stagecoach team turned out to be combination horses, broken to bridle or trace. This left the Danford bunch two extra mounts to use as *remuda* and pack animals.

Early on, Danford had expected trouble over the women—fighting among his men. But other troubles kept them occupied at first.

Almost as soon as they crossed into Mexico, they encountered a group of ragtag freebooters terrorizing travelers in the border country. Thanks to their captured Army carbine, Danford's gang were able to kill several horses and scare the marauders shy of them.

But there was also the constant threat from horse-stealing Comanches in this range. The Indians had learned it was far easier to steal a good horse than to capture green ones and break them.

On the grassy expanses near water, the wild mustangs themselves—"scrubs," as the gringos called them—were sometimes dangerous. Some had become man-killers and attacked, led by vicious, long-maned stallions. Once, Danford's gang was forced to set a hasty grass fire to drive off an aggressive herd too numerous to shoot.

"Jesus! I'm dried to jerky," Lorenzo complained toward the end of their busy second day in Old Mexico. "One of you greedy-gut bastards has been hogging extra water. Or else giving it to them society bitches."

Lorenzo rolled his head back in the direction of the two prisoners. They rode side by side behind him, each astride one of the blood bays stolen from the coach line.

"Fair trade, ain't it?" remarked Coyote in his flat monotone. "A sup of water for a sup of titty."

Despite their empty bellies and aching muscles, everyone except the women laughed at this. But Danford knew their water situation was no laughing matter. Even the most dependable desert dirt tanks were dry or nearly dry—nothing left but little tepid puddles full of dead bugs.

However, food, too, soon became a problem. The malnourished men had made short work of their

Judd Cole

beans and tortillas back at the way station. On that second day, toward sundown, Coyote shot a wild horse—a fat young colt.

He rough-gutted it and roasted it whole, brains and all, in a big, shallow pit, tossing in a few wild onions and some marrow fat to season it. Weevil-infested prison food had taught the gang to savor horse meat. But both women refused to eat it, or even to look at it.

Coyote watched the women, huddled at the far side of the fire pit. The air had cooled off dramatically after the sun went down. Coyote winked at the rest of the men.

"Mm-*mmm*!" he called out, making sure the prisoners could hear him well. "Ain't nothing touches roasted colt meat."

"Better than beef," Willard agreed with his mouth full, juice streaking off his chin. "Real tender."

"And easy pickin's?" Danford said. "Hell, a colt is so friendly it runs right up to a man just like a pup will! One good shot behind the ear."

"Use a hammer," Coyote suggested, "saves you the bullet."

"Shut *up!*" Connie Emmerick shouted at them, unable to bear this sick cruelty. "Can't you just eat it without all the crude gloating?"

"You best learn to stomach horse meat, ladies," Danford taunted them. "That's all there'll be."

"No," Coyote said quietly, standing up and wiping his greasy hands off on his shirt. "I believe tonight there's going to be something else on their plates."

Connie tried to make herself smaller as she saw the half-breed walking toward her, smiling his horrid turtle-mouthed smile. She knew he was part Yaqui

Yuma Bustout

Indian, a tribe of northern Mexico known for their fierce independence. Her husband had told her once the Yaquis were very different from the friendly, submissive tribes of central and southern Mexico.

Then again, Coyote must be very different from anyone, she feared, seeing the smoldering sickness in his eyes now that he was drawing so close. *All* these men frightened Connie terribly, but especially Fargo Danford and this mad Coyote. Neither brute, she was convinced, could take a woman without hurting her—hurting her bad. She could read meanness in a man's face, and Coyote's had it in spades.

"Hey? If Coyote is gettin' some," Lorenzo said, also standing up, "then by God, so'm I! Matter fact, I got first share on the young one. Damn me if I'll take leavings from a 'breed"

"First share, my ass!" Willard called out. "Make 'em snooty bitches choose the first bull to mount!"

Both women flinched hard when Danford's side arm spat a red fire-jet from its muzzle.

"Just hold it right there, boys!" he commanded in a tone of unquestionable authority. "I told each and every one of you when you joined up with me—it's *my* road or the high road! You've all seen what it's been like these two days on the run. Freebooters, Comanch, killer herds."

"Sure," Coyote said reasonably. "That's why we need a little fun now, see, boss?"

"Nope, I don't. Lissenup, all you! No foofaraw until we get to a safer place. We can't have *no* distractions, no fightin' 'mongst ourselfs, else we're all up Salt River! None of that sweet stuff until we get holed up near La Cola, hear?"

"I don't like that rule," Lorenzo complained.

Judd Cole

"Tough. I've seen this happen too often. The woman hunger gets in a man, it ruins his common sense. I've seen men kill each other fighting over whose goddamn turn it is! Just wait until we get the swag and got us a safe camp. You hear me, Coyote?"

"I hear you."

But Coyote finished crossing to the two women and knelt in front of them. Connie almost retched when she felt his leathery hand grip her chin. He forced her to stare into his bone-button eyes. He trailed a reek of rotgut whiskey, stolen from the dead coach driver.

"Maybe I'll cut you too, huh?" he whispered with sinister softness. "Take my use of you a few times, then just cut your pretty skin open from belly to throat, hanh? You being so famous, you can *act* like you're dying!"

A sob got past her will to resist him. It hitched in her chest, and Connie buried her face in her sister's velvet traveling jacket. Coyote laughed long and hard in the gathering darkness, then finally walked away.

Early the next morning, fate intervened to change Danford's plans.

Two hours after sunup, they were skirting a huge, irrigated *ejido*, or collective farm, at Weeping Woman Springs. Danford spotted a group of unarmed workers talking in a distant alfalfa field.

"Coyote, you talk good Mex," Danford said. "Ride over and find out why those dirt scatterers are jawing it like old ladies at a church social. Might be about us, so play it easy."

Coyote followed orders and soon returned. A tense

Yuma Bustout

glint had settled into his eyes—as if he didn't know whether to be angry or amused.

"What?" Danford demanded. "What the hell is it?"

"Could be a rumor," Coyote said.

"What, damn you!"

Coyote fired the word at him like a bullet. "Hickok!"

And like a bullet it struck. "Hickok?" he repeated woodenly, the force of it addling him.

"Sure. Those men say Mexican authorities are mad that the famous gringo has entered their country illegally to save two beautiful and famous women."

At first, hearing his enemy's name so abruptly spoken, Danford tasted the acidic bile of fear and rage. But that moment passed quickly. A warm glow of elation took its place.

"Good," he said with conviction. "This is our best chance, boys. Hickok's bragged for years now how he marched us to prison with empty shooters. They put it in the newspapers, even. Hell, our own families laughed at us for fools."

Danford took the lead again. "We'll still go to La Cola. But for now, we leave the silver be. Going near it's too damn risky until Hickok is planted deep."

"You seem cocksure," Lorenzo said, "that we *will* plant him. Plenty have tried."

"Sure. Tried it up north. That's Hickok's home range. This is Mexico. He's been down here before, but most of it's new to him."

Briefly, Danford explained about the time he was imprisoned for six months up in Santa Fe for beating a man so hard it left him crippled for life. While locked in the city *carcel*, Danford whiled the time by

Judd Cole

reading books about the old Spanish generals in Mexico. The ones who succeeded, he told his men now, always made damn sure they first established several haciendas as support bases.

"We'll take a lesson from them. See, Hickok can't trust a *priest* down here. Everybody down here knows about the reward that Texan put on Hickok for killing his son. Hell, his head's worth ten thousand Yankee dollars—that's a load of pesos!"

Coyote nodded, liking the sound of all this. "I take your drift. Hickok don't have no place he can rest. We do."

Connie felt her skin crawl as all four men turned to stare at her and Anne.

"And when we get to them rest places," Lorenzo said, speaking for all of them, "we'll have us some female comfort."

Chapter Five

"This border stretch spells trouble for any traveler," Bill explained to Josh. "The worst desperadoes from both countries are drawn here like flies to syrup. 'Law,' down here, is pretty much the gun and nothing else."

"Which means," Josh said, "it's especially dangerous for us because of that open reward on your head."

Bill nodded, his gunmetal eyes sweeping the barren landscape. Already, sun and dry wind had cracked his lips deep.

"Word is out that I'm over the border," Bill said. "Every two-penny gunsel in the area will be looking to cash in."

Hickok met Josh's eye and shrugged. "We all gotta die once," he remarked amiably. "But we don't have to rush it, so you're welcome to cut loose, kid. No sense *both* of us ending up in a nameless grave."

Josh tilted his hat against the progress of the broiling sun. "A grave's a grave, I s'pose. I ain't particular."

He reached for the canteen dangling by a strap from his saddle horn. Bill stayed his hand.

"Kid, you don't survive down here unless you play by careful rules. The first one is about water. *Never* drink when you're in the sun. It'll just turn to sweat before your body can use the fluid. One swallow in the shade is better than a quart hogged in the sun."

Reluctantly, Josh left the canteen alone. He had gotten his first nasty taste of North American deserts even before they crossed the border into Mexico near San Luis. Their private train from Denver could only take them, by way of a remote spur line of the Central Pacific Railroad, within seventy miles of Yuma. So they had ridden horseback the rest of the way.

"How'd you like Governor Jacobs and his cattle baron friend?" Josh inquired. They'd met both men briefly at Jim Paxton's luxurious ranch.

"The gov seems all right," Bill replied, "far as stump screamers go. But Paxton is a fool who somehow got rich. Worst kind. He might be trouble before we're done. He hates me on principle."

"A lot of men do."

"The way you say," Bill agreed.

The two men stopped at least once an hour to breathe the horses. The Danford gang's trail was hit and miss, depending on the drifting sand. But Josh realized Bill was hardly bothering to look down for sign. He obviously knew right where the group was aimed.

"Their bridles are pointed toward La Cola," he told

Yuma Bustout

Josh. "For one thing, they know damn good and well no sane man would follow them into that mare's nest."

"No sane man—but we will?"

Wild Bill's teeth flashed under his dusty mustache.

"Cowards to the rear, Longfellow! But I think the main reason they're heading to La Cola is because their swag is hidden around there. Nobody ever found it, far as I know."

The two friends slogged on. Josh felt tossed between twin horns: When he wasn't longing for water, he was battling saddle sleepiness.

His first night in the desert had shocked him. After daytime temperatures soaring well over a hundred degrees, the night had turned downright cold. Cripes, there'd actually been frost on his blanket roll in the morning! Following Bill's lead, Josh too had licked the morning dew off his saddle.

Josh was jogged back into the present moment when Bill called for another breather. Both men swung down, then threw their bridles. They fed their mounts handfuls of corn from their saddle pockets.

"Fire-away is holding up good so far," Bill remarked, watching his strawberry roan contentedly munch corn. "But actually a mule is what you want for crossing these deserts. I ain't never met any two horses could do the work of one mule. But then, a man can't get chummy with a mule. Their nature is against it. Well, back to the salt mines."

They covered another fifteen or so hard miles in loose, blowing sand. Finally Bill halted them in the lee of a wind-scrubbed knoll.

Josh watched Bill gaze toward the setting sun. He

lifted his hand out and squinted as he studied it, putting it between his face and the sky.

"What're you doing?" Josh demanded.

"There's four fingers left between sun and horizon. In the desert, that means about thirty minutes of light left. We best pitch camp."

Up north, Josh had noticed, the days generally bled into the nights, gradual and slow. But here in the desert, it got dark suddenly.

"We'll eat and grab some sleep," Bill decided. "No sentries but the horses. Then we'll ride out the night. There'll be a full moon tonight. Easy riding, so long's we watch for snakes."

Bill had smoked his rifle sights earlier and shot a plump antelope rabbit at two hundred yards. He quickly dressed it out while Josh built a cooking fire under a ledge to hold down the smoke.

"This La Cola," Josh said later while the two men gnawed charred meat under a star-spangled desert sky. "You been there before?"

Wild Bill shook his head. "Tell you true, the place scares me. I did get close once, trailing this same bunch the first time."

"Ned Buntline wrote an article about the place. Said if he owned La Cola and Hell, he'd rent La Cola out and live in Hell."

Bill laughed. "Usually, Buntline is full of sheep dip. But he struck a home truth when he said that. Kid, this ain't no 'town.' It's a rat hole, a snake pit, and a bear's cave, all rolled into one. They'll shoot or stab any stranger for his boots. Hell, for his *socks*."

"Well, then, doesn't sound like women—especially ladies—would stand a chance there," Josh mused, thinking of Anne Jacobs and Connie Emmerick.

Yuma Bustout

Using his saddle as a pillow, Bill stretched out. He drew both Colts and laid them nearby on his folded duster, ready to hand.

"Tell you the straight, kid," Bill finally replied from behind his hat. "Knowing the Danford gang like I do, I doubt if the women are still alive. And if they are, they won't want to be for long. That's why we have to hurry, the heat be damned."

"My lands!" Anne whispered to her sister. "That smell is going to make me ill!"

Connie, too, was sickened by the stink of the gang's heavy Mexican tobacco. All of it blew straight back to the rear of the group, where they rode. It was even stronger than cigar smoke.

Connie thanked God that, so far anyway, the worst still hadn't happened. Heat, hunger, thirst, exhaustion, an undignified loss of privacy, their captors' terrible smell and language—she would gladly endure all of it if only those stinking, subhuman beasts did not violate her or Anne! Connie was frightened, but stout in her spirit.

At least help was coming! Connie had little use for uncouth frontiersmen like J. B. Hickok. But these outlaws seemed to know and fear him. And that had kept them preoccupied with their safety, thank God.

The group had reached a place, in this horrible and desolate journey, that Danford called Los Estrechos, the Narrows. A spot where the ascending trail became a series of switchbacks, winding higher and higher from the flat desert floor through a rocky pass.

"Come on, Fargo!" Lorenzo complained as they finally cleared the pass. "Lookit what we just come through! Call a break, why'n't you?"

Connie did look back, and down the slope they'd just climbed. The full moon was bright enough to leave shadows from the wind-twisted cacti and stunted trees. That vast, moon-bleached landscape glowed an eerie whitish blue.

"Break? Buncha female men." Danford spat scornfully, but he did call for a breather.

"La Cola," he added as they dismounted, "ain't but a whoop and a holler away now. You goin' weak-kneed on me, boys? Hell, 'em stall-fed bitches complain less than you 'men.' "

The rest ignored him, stiff from the saddle. Connie and Anne averted their eyes as the men openly relieved themselves nearby.

Danford remained on horseback, watching everything with a cynical sneer. He shifted his gunbelt, threw a leg around the horn, and built himself a smoke.

"Coyote," he called out. "When you get done, best hark to our back trail. I don't trust Hickok."

Coyote nodded.

Now Danford dismounted. He walked over to the spot where both women huddled. He stood with his feet planted wide, thumbs tucked behind his shell belt.

"You," he said, staring at Anne. "I heard your man talk it up once in Bisbee, know that? Sure. He's one o' them play-the-crowd men. Common man's friend, all that hogwash. 'What's mine is yours, boys!' Well, now I've called his bluff, ain't I? And he don't seem to like turnabout when it's his woman."

"What I say," Willard suggested, his eyes stripping Connie. "We all take a whack at 'em now."

"Won't be long now," Danford promised him. "Just

hold your powder. First I want to be sure we ain't got Hickok on our tail."

"If Hickok is fool enough to go near La Cola," Lorenzo pointed out, "he's paring the cheese mighty close to the rind. It's only ten miles from here."

"Hickok's been known to go where he ain't safe."

Heat lightning flashed out on the horizon, though there was no chance of rain coming. Coyote, who had ridden down their back trail for a look, returned just as Danford gave the order to saddle up again.

"No trace of any trackers yet," he reported. "But there's an old man on a burro coming up the pass. Got a big poke sack with him."

"That'll most likely be an old fart named Esteban," Danford explained. He knew La Cola and its denizens better than did the others. "Prideful old fool, but smart. We'll pump him for information."

Esteban Velasquez was an ancient *curandero*, an herbalist who treated the sick and wounded of La Cola. A lifelong resident of this area, he had nonetheless remained honest to the bone. Esteban knew as much as anyone did about the constantly shifting power struggles in La Cola, where one criminal faction after another gained power over the rest.

Connie spotted the old man approaching from the crest of the slope. Tired eyes like old wounds peered out from the weathered grooves of his face. The old-timer smiled when he saw the two women.

However, Connie watched the smile fade when he spotted the men—especially Fargo Danford.

"Hola, viejo!" Danford greeted him. "What's going on, old man?"

Esteban clucked at his ancient burro, and the ungainly animal stopped. His saddle was an old wheat sack. Another big sack was tied around the old man's waist. The bottom bulged with leaves and roots.

"*Nada de particular*," Esteban replied in a hoarse, cracked voice.

He tried to ride past. But Danford grabbed hold of the burro's rope halter.

"Coyote!" Danford shouted. "You talk better Mex than me. Tell this old coot I want the goods on La Cola. Who's running the place these days, who's got liquor and guns and ammo, all that."

Coyote fired several questions at the old man in Spanish. But to each one, Esteban simply shook his head and responded "*No sé.*"

"Says he don't know nothing," Coyote finally told his boss.

"The old goat's a liar! Let's refresh his damn memory. Hold his burro, boys!"

Connie watched, heart pulsing hard in her throat, as Danford tied one end of a rope around the old Mexican's neck. He tossed the other over the gnarled branch of a mesquite tree.

"Talk out, old man!" Danford warned. "*Habla*, damn you!"

When Esteban still refused to cooperate, Danford backed up with the rope. He tied it to his horse's saddle. When Danford prodded the horse forward, it lifted the old man nearly off his burro, savagely choking him.

"Talk out!" Danford ordered again, letting Esteban down again.

Connie watched Esteban stare at his tormentor, then spit in contempt.

Enraged, Danford goaded his horse forward again.

Yuma Bustout

This time it pulled the rope so hard that Esteban was raised completely off his burro, choking hard.

"Stop it!" Connie pleaded, and Anne joined her. "Oh, please, *stop* it!"

Their pleas amused Coyote, who started laughing. But Danford, fleshy lips set tight in rage, ignored all of it.

Esteban's face turned purple, then black. His body jerked spasmodically like a fish on a hook. Horrified, both women begged Danford to let the old man down. By the time he did, however, it was too late.

Danford let go, and the dead man slid off his burro like a sack of grain.

Willard pounced on him, going through Esteban's pockets.

"When you get done there, Willie," Danford said, ignoring the dead man, "I want you to ride back up with me into the Narrows."

Willard stood up. "The hell for?"

Danford smiled in the silver-white moonlight.

"On account Hickok will be coming through there," Danford replied. "Sure as cats fighting, he'll be coming. And we're going to make sure he has him a little accident."

Coyote stared at both horrified women, grinning with sadistic pleasure. They were still staring at the old man's corpse.

"Gonna free Wild Bill's soul, ladies," Coyote told both women. "Like we just freed Esteban's."

Chapter Six

"Keep your nose to the wind," Bill warned Josh. "The old scouting days tell me this stretch coming up is going to get rough."

His voice slapped Josh out of his saddle doze. No more nascent moon. From the position of the polestar, which Bill had taught him to read, he guessed it was a couple hours before dawn.

"Man rough or nature rough?" Josh asked.

"Both, I'd guess, but mostly man. Stay awake, now."

The thick stands of ocotillo, numerous on the flatland, had thinned out as the trail wound and twisted its way higher. They passed through a stretch of desolate lava-bed country, then into the rough, folded hills beyond.

"What makes you get a hunch?" Josh asked.

"Kid, hunches are mostly *your* line of work. I bank

on experience. I was fighting outlaws while you were still on Ma's lap. Now, pipe down and stay alert."

At midmorning, the two men reined in. They stripped the blankets and rigging from their horses. After letting both grateful horses roll in the sand to bathe, they spread the wet blankets out in the sun to dry. Again the men shared parched corn with their mounts. Each animal also received a few meager swallows of water from their hats.

Bill studied the U.S. Army map Governor Jacobs had given him. He had followed a different route during his only other ride to La Cola, though he had taken this route back.

"This stretch coming up is called the Narrows," Bill told Josh. "So far, what we've ridden through is a Sunday school picnic compared with what it turns into higher up there. As I recall, we'll soon be seeing plenty of rimrock to hide bushwhackers."

"You really think they'll jump us this soon?" Josh demanded.

"Hell, you can take it to the bank! So stop pestering me with questions, kid."

"I'm doing my job is all!"

"So is a whore, but she can't do it uptown. Kid, don't argue with me right now—save it for later. I can't tell you where and when they'll make their play, but we better be ready when they do. Now, shut the hell up, or I'll gag you."

"Atta boy, Willie," Danford encouraged his partner. "Just a little bit more . . . there!"

Danford straightened up again and sleeved sweat off his forehead. He and Willard were exhausted after a hardscrabble climb up to this spot. About a hundred feet below them, the trail to La Cola formed a narrow shelf above a sheer cliff of stratified rock. Between this spot where they stood and the trail was a steep, scree-covered slope.

"Might herniate us pushing this pup over," Danford said, slapping a huge boulder. "But once she gets to rolling? Why, she'll take a few tons of slope rock with her. Anybody on that trail when it hits can kiss his sweet ass so long."

"Fargo, I'm beat out," Willard complained. "And we still got to climb down! Wouldn't it make more sense to shake Hickok off our tail with bullets 'steada bustin' our humps at donkey labor to make a rock slide?"

" 'Shaking Hickok off our tail' ain't the game, Willie. Shake off your cobwebs, boy! What's the good of dodging the fare if we lose our freight? If we don't kill him and be done with it, Hickok will hound us into the mouth of Hell! You ain't learned that by now?"

"All right then, damnit! Let's kill the son of a bitch. It's just, I'm tired and hungry and thirsty."

Willard edged forward and peered down toward the trail.

Danford swore and grabbed his arm, pulling Willard back.

"Hanchon, you're a bigger fool than God made you! When I said we have to kill Hickok, I didn't mean we want to go toe-to-toe with him. Don't ever give him a target like you just done."

"Ahh, I'm sick of this," Willard carped. "A man can't even cut the dust out here."

"You'll be in La Cola quick enough. They got 'em a pulqueria. You had pulque before and liked it fine. It's a good drink if a man can't have whiskey."

But Willard, like his brother, never lacked for gripes.

"That damn Lorenzo," he muttered, rubbing his sore tailbone. "He hogged the best horse. One I'm riding's got a rough gait. You can't—"

But Danford suddenly hushed him by raising one hand.

"Keep quiet," he whispered. "I hear 'em coming."

Josh fell silent when he saw how the rough trail had narrowed even more. To his right, a steep, rock-strewn slope rose toward the jagged rimrock; to his left, a sheer cliff dropped hundreds of feet to the pointed basalt turrets below.

Wild Bill rode about ten yards ahead of him, his eyes in constant motion. It was so cold now that the horses' breath rose in puffs of white steam.

Bill halted them often now, peering constantly overhead toward the rimrock. Josh also knew the former scout was sending his hearing out beyond the near distances. All Josh could hear was the muffled thud of the animals' hooves, the long, fluming snorts as they blew. But Hickok seemed to hear something else.

Wild Bill had felt this before: this sense that he was both participating in and observing his fate at the same time. It was just like a dream, only he knew this was the real world. And he knew that trouble was coming very soon now, perhaps in the next breath. His fabled guns were less valuable, right now, than his honed reflexes and quick reactions. But he mustn't miss the slightest clue.

Such as those few small pebbles just now trickling down the slope to his right. True, the movement was

Yuma Bustout

so slight a bird or scurrying insect might have caused it.

"Freeze, kid," he called back. "Hug the slope."

Immediately Josh reined in his piebald. Fire-away was trained to stop immediately whenever his reins touched the ground. Wild Bill tossed them forward, then drew his right-side Colt and stared straight overhead.

The solid mass of the slope gave way to deep indigo sky. Stars glowed like scattered crystals. But Bill's narrowed eyes detected a place where the dense pattern of stars seemed to be blotted out. As if by some object. It was right where the sky met the top of the slope.

And whatever that object was, it seemed to be moving.

This time, Bill didn't bother to hold his voice down.

"Kid, here's the elephant! Wheel and retreat! Rock slide!"

Even as Bill barked the command, he grabbed his reins and wheeled his horse around. Still looking overhead, he glimpsed a flesh-colored oval peering down toward the path.

Bill got off a quick snap-shot, his horse still wheeling, his body off balance in the saddle. Nonetheless, Hickok had the immediate satisfaction of hearing a man scream overhead.

Josh, too, was just starting to get his pony turned around when—*whumpf!*—a body rolled and crashed down hard onto the trail between him and Bill.

Wild Bill just had time to recognize Willard Hanchon's surly, death-startled face in the moonlight; puckered flesh on the forehead marked the bullet hole. But then, quick as a heartbeat, the entire slope above them was heaving downward in a rumble like an avalanche.

A liquid fear iced Bill's veins. He kicked Fire-away with both heels. Their only option now was to retreat far enough down their back trail. Otherwise, they'd be crushed on the trail or impaled on the basalt turrets far below.

"But even if we could get away," Anne Jacobs told her sister in a weary voice just above a whisper, "where would we go? And these filthy brutes have the only water. Dear, I hate to say it, but our only real choice is to pray that Wild Bill Hickok is more than just a dime-novel hero."

Connie nodded in the darkness, eyes trembling with the effort to fight back tears. Her sister was right, of course. No matter how hopeless their plight, running away was simply not an option. That's why Coyote and Lorenzo had not even bothered to tie up their captives.

The two women huddled together for warmth at one side of a mesquite-wood fire, now burned down to a few coals. This crude camp had been made on the south side of the Narrows. Fargo Danford and Willard Hanchon had gone back up to make some kind of trouble for Hickok.

Connie prayed with all her heart that their trap would fail. But the more immediate threat came from Coyote and Willard's brother, Lorenzo.

At first the two men had been too tired to trouble the women. They took turns sleeping and keeping an eye on their prisoners. But now both men were awake, smoking cigarettes and talking quietly as they cast continual glances toward Connie and Anne.

Yuma Bustout

They're about to do something, Connie realized, her pulse rapidly increasing.

Dear God, wasn't it awful enough already? Both women felt filthy and nerve-frazzled. They hadn't washed in days or had a decent meal, not to mention more than a few moments of stolen rest. And now this heart-hammering fear: not just of rape, but of what these sick men might do to hurt them, too.

And God have mercy, both men were walking toward them.

Coyote kicked at the glowing coals until flames illuminated both women.

"Let's see something nice," he ordered Connie.

Before she could make any move to stop him, he grabbed hold of her bodice and, showing no mercy, tore it loose. His grip tore the silk chemise away, too, exposing her breasts to the flickering light.

"Put your damn arms down," Coyote ordered her, for Connie had raised them to cover herself.

When Connie hesitated, Coyote calmly kicked Anne in the stomach. Connie screamed, begging him to stop, and dropped her arms. But she turned her face, crimson with humiliation and anger, away from the men's hungry, prodding eyes.

"Damn, man," Lorenzo finally said after swallowing audibly. "*Damn*. Lookit them nipples, Coyote! Look just like in 'em French paintings, don't they? Just like juicy plums."

"Sure. But I ain't one to look without having," Coyote told him. "Let's match coins. Winner tops her first."

"You can have her first," Lorenzo said in a burst of generosity, turning to Anne. She had just managed to get her breath back after Coyote's kick. "Thissen ain't no stable filly. But she'll do just fine."

"Please," Connie said. "Leave my sister alone. If you must . . . if . . . then, please just let it be me."

Coyote was already unbuckling his wide leather belt. "Spare us the noble blather. This is a two-course meal. *Both* you bitches look good."

Both women had spent much of their time praying. And perhaps they were being rewarded now. For suddenly everyone in camp heard the sequence of sounds clearly: a man's startled shout of warning, followed in a few seconds by a shot, then a bloodcurdling scream. Then they felt the ground tremble as the roaring, crashing din shattered the night.

"Somebody got killed, all right," Coyote told Lorenzo. "But who?"

He stared at the women. "This will wait. Saddle up, ladies. *Now*. We're moving down the trail."

Chapter Seven

Quick reflexes and superb horses saved Wild Bill and Josh from the tumbling mass of rocks that buried Willard Hanchon. The two riders, warned just in time, escaped down their back trail.

When the dust cleared, they picked their way over the moonlit rock heap and rode down out of the Narrows without further incident. Bill quickly read the signs at the abandoned camp.

"Two of 'em waited here with the women. They've just lit out toward La Cola."

Bill's eyes flicked back toward the Narrows. "And one dead. That means one of them is still up there. He might come this way, but he'll most likely take the long way down the south slope to avoid us."

Bill started to unsaddle his roan. "Either way, I'm too tired to flush him now. Be sunup soon. Let's take turns grabbing a little shut-eye. Then, God help us, we'll ride into La Cola."

Bill took the first watch. Two hours later, he woke Josh. Then, while the bleary-eyed journalist made notes in a flip-back pad, Bill slept like a dead man.

By the time Josh shook Hickok awake, the desert heat was already so thick it had weight. Ragged parcels of cloud drifted slowly across a deep blue dome of sky.

"God kiss me if I couldn't wrap my teeth around some hot eggs and scrapple," Bill said wistfully while he rigged his horse.

"Maybe there's a place to eat in town," Josh suggested.

Bill gave a scornful snort. "'Town'? Kid, I ain't been there. But I hear La Cola is a place to *be* the meal, not get one."

Both men ate a handful of parched corn and drank a few swallows from the last of their tepid water. Then they checked their weapons and swung up and over, reining their mounts southeast toward La Cola.

Now they were down on the flats again, the terrain arid and open. There was nothing but the occasional twisted Yucca tree or tall, narrow cactus called Spanish Bayonets by the locals.

Hickok's eyes never stopped scanning.

"Listen," he told Josh. "I know that Quaker ma of yours back in Philly taught you to always be polite. But *don't* be when you're in La Cola. This is Old Mexico. Just look bored and don't make eye contact with anyone. Down here, a man who smiles and says please and thank you is a weak sister. And weak sisters are killed for sport. Stick close to me."

"You kidding? I plan to. I ain't no hero."

Yuma Bustout

"That's one reason I like you, kid," Bill said. "You're scared, but by God that never keeps you in your tipi when the war whoop sounds, does it? You're a good man to have along."

It wasn't Hickok's way to lavish praise on a man. Josh knew these simple words came straight from the frontiersman's heart. They made the youth swell with pride.

But his first glimpse of La Cola deflated him and evoked something very different from pride.

Josh saw a handful of mud-colored adobe hovels, all of them small and wretched. Empty bottles, rusted cans, and various bones—animal and human—dotted the drab, barren sand around the buildings.

"No schools or churches," Bill said wryly as they rode slowly in, horses' hooves kicking up yellow plumes of dust.

The street was empty except for a little boy. He squatted in the shade of a building, eating a tortilla. He watched the two *norteamericanos* ride in, his face inscrutable.

None of the adobe hovels had signs advertising their business. But several included a few wooden cribs out back for whores and their customers.

Most of the hovels appeared empty and abandoned, but quite a few horses were hitched to a tie rail in front of the largest structure. Josh heard a wheezy accordion playing *"Una Paloma Blanca."*

"Welcome to your first pulque bar, kid," Bill said as they swung down. "Cactus liquor doesn't taste that bad. Just remember: It's the custom to take the first drink straight down. Don't pause until the cup is empty, or it's an insult."

Judd Cole

Bill whistled toward the little kid in the shade. When the boy had trotted over, Bill flipped him two bits.

"*Por guardar los caballos, niño.* That's for watching our horses, kid. I'll give you another when we come out."

The kid bit the coin, then grinned. "*'Sta bien, señor!*"

Bill stepped through the open doorway into the hot, smoky, sweat-stinking dimness within, Josh close on his heels. The young reporter, heart hammering his ribs, received a quick impression of the desert watering hole.

There was no bar, just a raw plank counter supported by several sawhorses. There were no tables or chairs, either, just a few crude three-legged stools, though most of the patrons were standing or leaned against the walls.

And *what* patrons! Josh felt his scalp break out in sweat at first sight of these raffish toughs in sombreros and serapes. Clay-colored and stoic-faced, not one was unarmed. Those who didn't carry firearms wore machetes in shoulder scabbards. These were men, Josh realized in a glance, who'd been bone-idle most of their lives except for brief moments of violence.

The music, and all conversation, fell silent as the two gringos entered. Bill strolled straight up to the counter and slapped it.

"*Dos copas,*" he ordered from a huge bartender with a fat and folded face.

Josh felt every man in the room staring at the new arrivals. The bar dog filled two chipped clay cups with the milky *pulque*. Josh remembered Bill's warning and drank the pungent, but not unpleasant, liquor straight down. It burned and made his eyes water, but he managed not to cough.

After finishing his cup, Hickok made quite a show out of pressing his fist into his stomach until he belched loudly.

"Custom of the country," he explained quietly to Josh, who followed this example.

That seemed to lessen the tension some, Josh noted gratefully. A few of the patrons were conversing again, ignoring the new arrivals.

"*Otra vez*," Wild Bill told the bar dog, who filled their cups again.

"You can drink this one slower," Bill told Josh. "Well, no sign of the Danford gang in here. Doesn't mean we won't hear something about them if we listen in good. Especially since they've got two good-looking women with them."

Josh risked a quick glance around. "Thank God it's dark in here. I don't think anybody recognizes who you are."

But Bill didn't bother replying, for trouble was indeed heading his way. A big Mexican wearing the leather chaps of a *vaquero* was swaggering toward the new arrivals. He greeted them in English.

"Welcome to La Cola, *hombres*! Where every man has a set on him and every woman says yes. I am called Reynaldo!"

Bill nodded. The *pulqueria* fell silent again. Josh could feel every man in the room watching them with the expectation of patrons at a cockfight.

"As you can see, *señors*," Reynaldo said with false unction, mixing English with enough Spanish so the rest could follow him. "La Cola is a quiet and uneventful place, *verdad*? We like to liven up our little *pueblito* with some friendly sport."

Reynaldo suddenly smacked the plank counter. Josh had to catch his cup when it leaped up.

"*Qué dices, amigo?* What do you say to a little arm-wrestling contest?" Without hesitation, Bill nodded again. This evoked laughter and remarks because Reynaldo, Josh estimated, easily had forty pounds on Bill. But Josh knew that Hickok, though lean in the shanks and stomach, carried most of his strength in his chest and arms.

Both men squared off in front of the counter, planting their elbows. The rest all crowded in closer, making Josh squirm. He could feel their collective heat, smell their collective odor.

"Miguel!" Reynaldo called out to the barkeep. "Where are Pinchito and Chispe? We cannot fight without our little friends, huh?"

Josh's eyes widened in revulsion and fear when Miguel reached under the counter and produced a fruit jar containing two black, squirming objects: scorpions! The barkeep opened the jar and shook one out near each man's arm.

The legs had been carefully tied together with string so the creatures couldn't move very far. Miguel lined them up so that whichever man began to win the match would force his opponent's arm closer and closer to the poisonous stinger at the tip of the scorpion's upraised tail.

If this dangerous turn of events surprised Hickok, he didn't show it. The two men gripped hands, and the contest was on.

Reynaldo wasted no time. He loosed a mighty roar, clearly expecting to defeat his man on the spot. And

Yuma Bustout

in fact, his first massive exertion did start to swing Hickok's arm down. Bill stopped it only an inch from the poison stinger. Josh bit his lower lip until he tasted blood.

When his first showy exertion failed, Reynaldo settled in to a determined effort. But that big exertion had cost him. Now Wild Bill's slow, steady determination was literally gaining the upper hand.

Sweat oozed from Reynaldo's face, and the veins in his neck bulged fat as night crawlers. Slowly, steadily, Bill muscled him down until only a fraction of an inch separated the Mexican from the stinger. Though usually not fatal for an adult, a scorpion's sting left a man terribly ill and weak—which, down here, could indeed be a fatal condition.

So this was the moment of truth. Reynaldo could choose his pride and keep struggling—until that stinger would surely inject him. Or the Mexican could just surrender completely, crushing the scorpion when Bill forced him down.

Reynaldo chose surrender. But he was also a poor loser, and a man given to keeping accounts. He watched Miguel brush the dead scorpion off the bar. Then Reynaldo stalked wordlessly off to join his friends again.

A few of the older locals had cheered when the plucky gringo triumphed. Nonetheless, Josh could feel it in the air—the unexpected victory caused a stirring of anger and resentment. Among most of these men, bitter memories of the unjust war caused by the gringos were still too sharp.

Besides all that, this den of thieves and murderers did not require reasons for seeking violence. It was the local form of entertainment.

"Time for us to ride on, Longfellow," Bill suggested quietly. He flipped four bits American onto the counter to cover their drinks.

But the look Miguel gave them was clear: Payment was not necessary, for he would be taking it from their pockets shortly. Though he clearly respected the stranger in the black hat, Miguel considered him as good as dead already.

"Get beside me, kid," Bill said, "and don't look at anybody. You got a story to file. Big byline, all that glory. That's it, son, eyes front."

The two men were halfway to the door before at least a half-dozen men moved to block it.

"Two sons of whores!" Reynaldo shouted in English behind them.

Josh felt his throat close with fear. Bill turned and gave Reynaldo the shadow of a smile.

"It is common knowledge," he announced clearly in Spanish, "that *I'm* your father."

No greater insult could be hurled at a Mexican male, for it clearly vilified one's mother while also insulting the father.

Reynaldo snarled and grabbed for the big dragoon pistol in his belt. Josh saw at least two other side arms coming up to the ready. He himself had his pinfire revolver halfway out of its holster.

However, he never had to fire it. Quicker than a finger snap, both Hickok's fists filled with iron. The right-hand gun bucked once, the left gun twice. And before any man present could credit his eyes, three dead men lay on the floor—all drilled dead center in the forehead.

"In a crowd situation like this," Hickok explained calmly to Josh, as if they were in a classroom, "I always prefer a head shot. Some men are partial to the heart. But I've found that some reptiles will still fight from reflex without a brain shot."

Now that Hickok's ivory-grip Colts were out from beneath his duster, the shocked patrons took a closer look at this steel-eyed *yanqui*.

"*Virgin de Guadalupe!*" exclaimed Miguel, making the sign of the cross. "Wild Bill Hee-kok!"

Bill wagged both smoking guns toward the men blocking the doorway. "Some men never learn. So they die ignorant. Make a hole, boys, or I'll blast one through you."

He spoke in English, but no one required a translation. The men fell back, tripping over each other in their haste.

"Just keep moving, kid," Bill said quietly. "And keep that gun out, that's the lad. Hold it right out plain. See, the shock will wear off quick. Then these jackals are going to remember that reward."

Chapter Eight

"It's all here," Fargo Danford announced triumphantly. "All thirty bars. Didn't I tell you boys this was a perfect spot? Sure, there's a couple Indians know about it, but they're long gone from here."

Danford climbed up out of an eight-foot-by-four-foot brick-lined enclosure. Located in the base of a small knoll just south of La Cola, the brick chamber had once served as a secret powder magazine for peasant rebels.

Danford whipped the dust from his hat and took a careful look all around them. This spot was well protected from sight by several abutments of rock. One had to leave the main trail to even suspect it might be here.

"We'll leave it right where it is," Danford added, "until we put Hickok with his ancestors. We cover our tracks good when we ride out from here, he'll never have any good reason to ride up here."

"When we ride out," Lorenzo repeated, his tone sarcastic. "Ride out to where?"

"Simmer down, bawl-baby. I got a place in mind. A good spot where Hickok can't surprise us. A gun hand like him catches us flat-footed, we're under. Look what he just done to your brother. That fool Willard gave him a one-second target, and Hickok plugged him."

"So you tell it," Lorenzo said quietly.

Danford's fleshy lips formed a scowl. "You wanna spell that out plain?"

"How plain is this? You *say* Hickok killed Willard, and maybe he did. But with both us Hanchon boys dead, you could split that silver with your favorite, Coyote, now couldn't you? Two shares 'steada four."

"You damned fool!" Danford laughed, harsh and loud. "You heard what Miguel said! Hickok gunned down Reynaldo and two of his gang in Miguel's place, drilled all three right in the brainpan! You think a man that gun-handy couldn't drop a simpleton like Willard, who didn't have the common sense God gave an ant?"

Coyote chimed in, his voice flattened of all emotion, yet menacing. "Lorenzo flaps his mouth too much. That was his brother's problem, too."

"Miguel said Hickok's not alone," Danford added, sliding the wooden cover back into place atop the cache of silver. "Got some fuzz-faced city kid with him, wears ready-to-wear boots."

"Prob'ly an ink-slinger," Lorenzo guessed. "They cover Hickok like flies on cow plop."

All three men were busy covering up the magazine

with sand and rocks. The spot was well sheltered from the force of the wind.

"I know that," Danford said. "Especially now on account of the women. Don't forget, boys, when it comes to money, Jacobs is rolling in it. So's Paxton. Could be a lot more profit in store for us, we play our cards smart."

All three men finished their task and circled out from behind the knoll. Their captives sat together in the scant shade cast by their tethered horses, miserable in the late-morning heat.

"Matter of fact," Danford said, stopping beside the women's horses, "maybe we best start taking better care of our female guests, boys. These is what you call assets."

"Mister, I *love* how their ass sets," Lorenzo quipped.

Coyote grinned. "You're funny when you ain't bawling."

"What I mean," Danford insisted, "is that a well-fed slave fetches more on the auction block. Matter of fact . . ."

Danford smirked at the captives. "I'm shortening your stirrups, ladies, so you'll be more comfortable as you tour Mexico with us."

Coyote giggled again. He crossed to where Connie sat hugging her knees. He squatted on his ankles, bringing his face close to hers. He had lately become fascinated by a vein that pulsed visibly in Connie's slim white throat. He watched it now.

"Well, howdy, Little Miss Pink Cheeks. You miss me?" His voice was a razor-thin whisper. "Won't be long now, little pretty. We'll make camp. Then you two ladies can get out of them wrinkled and dirty clothes, eh?"

Connie averted her face from this stinking, leering mask of lust and cruelty. Stoically, she watched a lone eagle soar over a distant peak. Its freedom mocked her, especially as she listened to Anne crying softly beside her.

"Grab some saddle!" Danford called out. "Like Willard found out, Hickok ain't down here to wash bricks. He's looking to kill us! Let's get a safe camp set up."

Three days' hard ride north of La Cola, in his stone-and-timber ranch house near Yuma, Jim Paxton met behind closed doors with a trail-hardened frontiersman named Butch Jeffries.

"I don't credit my own ears, Jim," Jeffries commented when the rancher finished speaking. "You can't be serious?"

Paxton stood with one elbow leaning against the mantel of a big fireplace that was seldom lit. A young Mexican maid, who spoke only a few words in English, hovered nearby with a decanter of whiskey and a feather fly-swisher.

"Am I serious? Serious as cancer," Paxton replied. "What? Is this job too rough for your belly?"

Jeffries shook his head. He was comfortably sprawled in a blue chintz easy chair. The walls behind him were lined with leather-bound books from floor to ceiling.

"It's not that," Jeffries assured him. "Especially right now. You've caught me when I'm a bit light in the pocket. I'll do it if you're sure it's what you want."

"Hell, you think I don't know my own mind?"

Jeffries shook his head. "Course you do. But this

Yuma Bustout

is . . . well, you know. Romance, or what you call it. You cool off and change your mind—"

"May I be damned if I'm not sure!"

Jeffries surrendered with a nod and killed the whiskey in his glass. He had a small, sharp, intelligent face. Few men wore two guns, and even fewer tied them down as Butch did. He was a former Army dispatch rider turned "businessman's agent." The private troubleshooter had spent the past fifteen years riding the border badlands.

"All right, then," Jeffries said. "It just sets me back on my heels a mite, is all. I mean, 'pears to me like you've drawn a circle around the prettiest girl in America. Now you want me to make sure she's dead?"

"Damnit, Butch, you still don't take my meaning! Her looks are nothing to the matter! She won't be worth having after this, yet by law and duty I'm now bound to honor the marriage. If those tainted scum in Danford's gang haven't raped her by now—repeatedly—Hickok will surely seduce her."

Jeffries grinned. "What if he does? A good pie is just as tasty with a few slices missing."

"That reasoning may be fine for the common run of mankind, but not for Jim Paxton. I won't abide spoiled goods, I'm telling you."

"You place too high a price on virginity, Jimbo. Personally, I like a gal what knows how to wiggle her hips."

"It's more than that! I'm already a pathetic cuckold, to hear the newspapers tell it. Every time Hickok even gets close to a pretty woman, the newspapers and magazines parade it. They're doing it already. Listen to this dreck."

Paxton crossed to a rolltop desk and snatched up that week's edition of the *Yuma Recorder*.

" 'Jim Paxton has indeed hired the best man for the job,' " he read. " 'But considering Miss Emmerick's striking beauty, is he perhaps sending a wolf to comfort the lamb? Wild Bill Hickok's penchant for female thespians is legendary. Nor have they, in turn, shown severe reluctance to encourage his zeal.' Good Lord!"

Paxton crumpled up the newspaper and threw it toward the maid. For a moment, rage gripped him so tightly it left his jaw aching.

But a moment later he was calm again. Judging from the maid's fearful eyes, Paxton's equanimity was even more dangerous than his rage.

"She's probably already dead by now," he told Butch. "It's tragic and all that. But in case Hickok does rescue her, your job is to make sure she doesn't make it back. I *won't* marry her! Can you imagine how this will look to history—what a pathetic fool I'll look?"

History? Hell, you look that way now, Jeffries thought. But he only nodded.

"My wife—the mother of my children—will inherit an empire after I die. And she *must* be pure."

Jeffries nodded again. "What the hell. It's your money, and I'm just a jobber. The pay's fine with me, so I'll leave tomorrow."

Chapter Nine

"It's water," Hickok said in a dubious tone. "And it's not poison, or the birds wouldn't be drinking it. The horses can drink it."

"Can we?" Josh demanded.

"In moderation. But I'll warn you right now, Longfellow. It'll likely give us the squitters."

"So? I've had *them* since we left Yuma."

Bill grinned.

Josh knelt beside the little muddy swale they'd followed the birds to. Bill claimed his Army map showed there was an underground river here, that this was a seep spring where pressure forced some water up through the ground.

Trouble was, the water leached through alkali dirt on its way through the soil. The brackish water had a bitter taste and left annoying grit in the mouth. For many, this grit also irritated the bowel.

Both men filled their canteens, then let their horses drink. It was close to noon on the day following their narrow escape from La Cola. By now both men looked rough and tired. Reddish-blond bristles stubbled Bill's cheeks, and even Josh had some dark whiskers on his upper lip. They both watched the barren, glaring desert from red eyes swollen halfway shut.

While the horses tanked up, their riders checked the animals for saddle galls. Bill fished a hoof pick out of one pocket and removed a few small stones from the roan's hooves. He also kept a close eye on the horizons, watching for any dust puffs. They were now the two most wanted men in Mexico. Actually, Bill was wanted, and Josh, he often reminded his companion, "would catch some of the extra bullets."

"Their trail's not been hard to pick up," Hickok told Josh as they rode out again, bearing southwest by the sun. "The problem is to hold it in this open country without being spotted. That means we have to get creative, kid."

Bill indicated the vast, open country with a sweeping gesture.

"It ain't smart to just lock on their trail and sniff their butts like hounds. They're deliberately pushing through the open flats. We've got to study the map, then try to guess where they'll end up. That way, we can get there by our route, not theirs. Keep a lower profile. Keep control of the situation, too."

Bill frowned, liking this terrain around them less and less. He had scouted open country enough to know that no ground anywhere was ever truly level, that a man could almost always find hollows and sinks, hummocks and folds, for some kind of cover.

Yuma Bustout

But this expanse of the Sonora seemed to have been shaken out like a tablecloth.

"I sure feel sorry for those women," Josh remarked.

"They're in a dirty corner, all right," Bill agreed. "But then, so are we."

Sweat beaded on Josh's forehead, and he took that as a good sign. He wasn't seriously dehydrated yet.

"Wish to God we could *do* something for them," Josh persisted.

"You young fool! We ain't the Knights of Malta, but what the hell are we doing right now?"

"Mostly eating dust."

"Sure," Bill argued, "because the best thing we can do right now is keep Danford and his cronies on the run. We keep them nerve-frazzled, worried about their own hides. A man who's ducking bullets ain't got time, nor inclination, to spend his lust."

Bill seemed to pronounce this from the depths of experience.

"This way," Hickok added, "we stay in control. We pick them off until they break and run. And if we get lucky, they leave the women behind as too much trouble."

Bill spread his map open across the saddle horn and studied it while Fire-away trotted. Josh knew he was putting his new plan to work: trying to guess, based on their trail so far, where the gang would choose to rest.

"There's volcano hills about twenty miles from here," Hickok finally said, looking up again. "That means water. I'd wager they're heading that way to rest."

Bill studied the terrain through slitted eyes.

"No use," he finally admitted. "Since I can't sight us

a route with better cover, let's hole up until night's coming on."

The two men took what shelter they could in the lee of a big dune, staking out their ground sheets for shelters.

They fed their horses the last of the parched corn, then picketed the animals in the scant shade of the dune.

Bill slid his Winchester .44-40 from its saddle boot and quickly checked the firing mechanism for sand. He had not kept a round in the chamber because of possible "cook offs" from the direct sun. He racked one in now.

"I'll take the first watch, kid," he said wearily. "Wake you up in a couple."

The spot was ideal for anyone on the run in this desolate stretch of northern Mexico: a long rock shelf located halfway up the slope of an otherwise nondescript lava hill.

From the desert floor below, the shelf appeared to be just another rock spine. But a climb upward soon revealed a big, natural chamber formed by erosion under the shelf. The area was as big as a ballroom, which left plenty of room for horses and people. And it included perpetual pools of cool, clean seep water.

Connie and her sister had mixed feelings about finally reaching this place. Their captors had actually allowed both women to bathe in private in a natural stone cistern at the back of the cavern. Even without soap, it felt wonderfully refreshing just to be wet and cool again.

But how long would the gang's "courtesy" last? There was only one good reason why the women had been left alone so far: The men were all too busy watching for Hickok.

Now, however, as the two women huddled together fixing each other's hair with pins, Fargo Danford appeared in the entrance, holding a dead rabbit. Blood still oozed from a wound in its side.

He walked back closer to the seated captives and threw the bloody carcass in Anne's lap. He tossed down a knife, too.

"Gut that son of a bitch, Mrs. Gov'nor," he ordered. "Save out the heart and kidneys—Coyote likes to chew 'em up raw."

Anne made a sound of distress in her throat, knocking the awful thing out of her lap.

"S'matter?" Danford demanded. "You too fine-haired to clean what you eat? Do like I said or go hungry, fancy woman. No skin off my ass."

Lorenzo walked back, too, and tossed a battered metal pan at Connie. She had to duck her head quick to avoid being struck with it.

"You! Juliet! Scrape the gravy skillet! We're starved here, damnit."

While the women went reluctantly to work, Danford and Lorenzo walked back to the cavern entrance, joining Coyote on watch.

"See how it is?" Danford said, his tone confident. "You can see from here to China and back! Even after the sun sets, there'll be a full moon."

All three men stood under the rock outcrop, sharing the last of their tobacco. A long, open slope led up to them, offering no cover larger than a few scrub weeds and small rocks. There was perhaps another hour before nightfall.

"Long as we all take watches," Danford assured

them, "nobody will sneak up on us. Besides, way that wind's raisin' hell, it might wash out our trail completely. Hickok might never find this place."

"Lotta people looking to pop Wild Bill," Coyote agreed. "The longer we keep him out in the open, the better our chances of getting out of Mex with our swag."

Lorenzo glanced back inside the cavern. "What about them, huh? You still hot to put a ransom on 'em?"

"Why not? But it's pointless until everybody knows we've put Hickok under. Us or somebody. I ain't particular who kills the son of a bitch long as it gets done."

"Sure," Lorenzo said, hardly listening. Now he was staring hard back into the cavern, his breathing quickening a little.

"Say, Fargo," he cajoled. "Like you said, from here we can see into China. What say we make tonight the night we have us some fun with 'em society gals?"

"The man's right," Coyote agreed in his atonal voice. "It's been put off too damn long now, Fargo, and you know it. You're wanting one of them, too."

"Both of 'em," Danford admitted.

"Works out real nice," Lorenzo said. "One man on watch leaves two men and two women. What say, boss? Think o' all them nights in prison without a woman."

Danford again gazed down the long slope, mulling the decision. After all, with Willard dead, that left one less man to fight over shares of the women.

Finally he nodded. "Tonight," he agreed. "After we eat. But lissenup, Coyote, no knifework when you finish, hear me? These two ain't like that whore you cut to ribbons in Matamoros."

Oh yes they are, Coyote thought. But he only nodded obediently.

"No knifework," he promised. "Just fun."

By late afternoon, Wild Bill and Josh had slept enough to function for a few more hours.

"Kid, grab a big rock and come with me," Bill ordered. "Before we ride out, I need some meat, damnit."

"Can't we just shoot it?"

"Could," Bill replied. "But you got any idea how far sound travels over a desert? No sense announcing we're coming."

"Where we going?" Josh demanded as they moved out from the protection of the sand dune. Josh had picked up a rock twice the size of his fist.

"Hunting," Bill replied tersely. "Shut up."

Bill carried his rifle, but he had it by the barrel, not the stock. Josh saw his eyes sweeping across the surface of the sand.

"There," Bill said. "Fresh track. Let's follow it."

"That's a snake's trail!" Josh protested.

"Rattlesnake, to chew it fine. Get ready with that rock, kid. We ain't far behind it."

Josh was about to fire off another question, but Bill suddenly lunged forward, pinning something in the sand. Only then did Josh hear the angry buzzing of the snake. It writhed furiously under the rifle butt, trying to escape.

"Hell, kid, you bolted down?" Bill demanded. "Smash its goddamn head before it bites me!"

The head, at least, was fairly still. Josh crushed it with one drop.

"Good work, kid," Bill said, his mood improving at the thought of hot meat. He tossed the dead snake over his shoulder.

"You roust up some mesquite wood," he told Josh. "I'll butcher us out some snake steaks."

"Don't know if I can eat that," Josh said.

"Ahh, you'll like it, kid. Tastes just like alligator."

It was dark enough now to risk the smoke from a fire if it was built in a pit. When Josh finally bit into the tender meat, he did like it.

"Didn't I say it tasted like alligator?" Bill asked.

"I never had that. But I could swear this is chicken."

"Chicken?" Bill said. "Don't believe I've ever tried it, kid. What's it taste like?"

"Just like rattlesnake," Josh assured him.

"I'll be damned."

While they ate, Bill studied his map in the dying light.

"I've been doing a process of elimination," he explained. "If we go on the assumption they want to head west by northwest, which is the way they're sticking, then there's only one logical destination."

Bill tapped the map with his index finger. "There's a place marked Devil's Shelf on the map. The cartographer has used the symbol for a cave to mark it."

"How far from here?" Josh asked.

"I think we can be close in about two hours. But we'd have to leave the horses for the final approach, go in on foot."

Bill washed his hands in the sand, his eyes meeting

the reporter's. "This won't be pretty, Longfellow. You'd best wait behind with the horses."

"That an order?"

Bill shook his head. "I don't coddle any man. You know the way of it, kid. What you choose to do is your show."

"Not really. I gotta go, or else how can I claim to be telling your story to millions of people?"

"There's still green on your antlers! Ned Buntline made a fortune off my name and never broke a sweat."

"Well, I ain't him."

"No," Bill agreed, pushing up to his feet. "You're twice the man he was, so you'll prob'ly die poor. Saddle up, kid, it's time to ride."

The horses, sensing water ahead, easily held a canter across the now dark, but still well lit, desert. It wasn't long before both men saw the rolling shadows of the lava hills out ahead.

They watered the horses at a seep spring, then left them hobbled in a *barranca*. Josh had watched Bill pocket some charred wood from their cooking fire. Now he realized why as Bill used it to smudge both their faces.

"Bright moon tonight," he explained. "This'll cut reflection."

Bill took his Winchester, filling his shirt pocket with extra rounds. "We'll move in on foot until we hit the slope," he said. "From there it's a low crawl the rest of the way. Cover will be scarce, but stick as close to me as you can—I've got the rifle. The plan is simple: I mean to shoot at the first target of opportunity."

Judd Cole

* * *

When their meal was over, Danford and Coyote went back out front of the cavern, where Lorenzo had drawn first shift on sentry duty.

"Hell," Lorenzo teased them, "you boys bashful? I'm damned if I mean to waste *my* turn with them beauties."

"Chuck that butt, you damn fool," Fargo snapped at Lorenzo. "You're giving Hickok a lighted target!"

"Ease off, I'm covering it with my hand. Ain't nothing down there anyhow."

But Danford made sure himself, studying each section of the wide slope for both shape and movement. After a long search, he finally nodded.

"Looks safe," he conceded. He turned to stare at Coyote. Both men grinned.

"Time to spark our ladies?" Danford said.

Lorenzo inhaled a last drag from his cigarette and flipped the butt away in a wide, glowing arc.

"Save some for me," he said. "Lucky bast—"

The bullet arrived a fraction of a second before the sound of the rifle. It punched into Lorenzo's right cheek and out his left, destroying teeth and gums and shattering one eye socket.

"Christ!" Bloody chips of tooth sprayed Danford's face. He and Coyote hit the ground even as another rifle slug whanged into the opening under the rock shelf.

Lorenzo had not been killed, which would have been more merciful. Now the pain of his hideous wound struck him full force before shock could numb it.

The howl he unleashed unnerved both his companions. The marksman below could easily have finished off Lorenzo; instead, he was evidently leaving him to work at the other two's nerves.

The plan succeeded. After twice telling Lorenzo to shut up and cover down, Danford simply shot him to put him out of his misery.

Danford and Coyote lay flattened, easing back under the shelf.

"See him?" Danford whispered.

"Nothing," Coyote replied.

"It's Hickok," Danford said. "Has to be."

This was confirmed a moment later when a familiar voice—relaxed, amiable, only slightly mocking—called out to them from the night.

"That's two down and two to go, boys. Sweet dreams. I'll be watching you."

Chapter Ten

"Steady on, kid," Bill whispered down to Josh. "Something's coming. They just don't know how to play it yet."

Josh had ridden with Bill long enough to conquer the worst of his fear. But watching Lorenzo die so horribly, slaughtered by his own men, had left Josh feeling like he'd been kicked hard in the guts. It reminded him that Danford's gang were not men at all but reptilian killing machines.

As if Bill, too, were thinking similar thoughts, the older man added: "I tried for a clean head kill, but I pulled it by two inches. Then, when I tried to throw a finishing shot into him, he was dancing all over. I ain't no Annie Oakley with a rifle."

Josh knew Bill meant it. He had never seen Hickok shoot at a man unless he meant to kill him quick with one shot. Still, the sound of Lorenzo's voice when the

Judd Cole

pain and realization struck him . . . Josh was a Christian, but he couldn't help wondering if the Indians weren't right, and the last moment of your life was the one you lived forever in the afterworld.

There was still no reaction from the cave. Josh found it hard to believe how quickly Bill had found *just* enough cover to sneak up the slope this far—perhaps a hundred yards from the rock overhang. With Josh almost literally on his heels, Bill seemed to sense the lowest ground with his body.

Josh now pressed into a low swelling of dirt that hid much of his body from view above. Bill lay just ahead, using no ground cover at all. He had merely pressed into a runoff seam, bringing his body just below ground level when he pressed flat.

Josh flinched hard when Bill suddenly shouted, "Danford? Make you a deal. Turn the women loose, I'm off your trail! Take your silver and cash in, it's none of my dicker! I just want the women."

"Don't you always?" a mocking voice called back. "Thanks for giving us a target, Goldilocks!"

Bill's voice gave the men a general direction to attack, and they opened up with a vengeance. A bullet whapped in so close it kicked sand into Josh's eyes. Another whumped into the mound of dirt protecting him.

In all, perhaps ten shots were fired, most of them striking very close by. But as soon as the guns above fell silent, Bill whispered confidently to Josh, "Don't sweat it, kid. That was just meant to panic us into moving so they'd get a better target."

"It almost worked, 'cept I was too scared to move."

"They won't do it again," Bill predicted. "They're sparing their ammo—they must be low."

Yuma Bustout

That made Josh suddenly worry about their own supply.

"Bill? I only have six cartridges."

"We're all right. I got a full belt for my short irons and a box of .44 rimfires in my saddlebag for the Winchester."

But soon Josh had something new to worry about: The mound of dirt behind which he was hiding suddenly emitted a hissing jet of steam.

Despite their precarious plight, Bill abruptly chuckled. "Kid, you're hugging a fumarole!"

Josh felt his heart skip a beat. Man alive, a fumarole! He knew they dotted Mexico, open vents over pockets of bubbling magma. Many were still active. The idea of being boiled alive made a bullet seem almost like a blessing.

"Shouldn't we move?" asked a nervous Josh.

"What, and give those buzzards up there clear targets? Kid, you're going simple on me."

"So what do we do, just stay here all night?"

"If we do, least you'll have heat. But don't worry," Hickok assured him. "I know Fargo Danford. Anything erupts around here, it'll be him. We won't have to wait long."

"Hold your fire, damnit!" Danford snapped at Coyote. "We ain't got enough ammo to just be shootin' at shadows!"

Coyote holstered his side arm and moved back farther under the rock ledge with Danford. Each man also carried a shotgun in case Hickok rushed them.

"So much for your goddamn 'safe haven,'" Coyote growled at his friend.

"You know a better place? Hellfire! A rabbit

couldn't get up that slope without showing itself. You said so yourself, Coyote."

Danford walked back into the big chamber to make a quick check on the women. Then he joined Coyote again.

"Look," Danford said. "If we ain't sleeping, Hickok ain't neither! He ain't got the upper hand, or we'd be dead! All we got to do is play it smart."

Coyote moved back outside, quickly checked the slope, then ducked in again. He was careful to stay low.

Danford moved close to the opening.

"Hey, Hickok?" he shouted. "You're a funny man, ain'tcha? Funny as a crutch! We got somethin' to make *you* laugh!"

"Coyote," he said, lowering his voice. "Bring me the governor's whore. And bring me a stick from the fire. Make sure you tie the other one up."

Coyote grinned like a schoolboy. He saw where this was going. "Now you're whistling, boss."

"Hickok!" Danford shouted. "I know you're a ladies' man, too! We got a gal here wants to say howdy!"

When Anne came forward, she was putting up no resistance—not with the point of Coyote's ten-inch knife tickling the bumps of her spine.

However, she began struggling in earnest when Danford brought a still-burning chunk of mesquite toward her right arm.

"No!" she begged. "Oh, please dear God, *no!*"

"Yes, damn you to hell!" Danford shot back.

With Coyote restraining her, Anne quickly ran out of room to retreat, and the flaming wood struck her forearm.

Yuma Bustout

Her scream, as Danford held it there, unrelenting, spread out into the desert night like the shriek of a dying puma.

"That was the governor's woman!" Danford shouted down to the attackers on the slope. "She's got her a brand-new scar for life, compliments of Wild Bill Hickok, the noble goddamn ladies' man!"

Josh was not a cussing man. But hearing Anne Jacobs suddenly cry out in terrible pain was more than he could bear in silence.

"Damnit, Bill, we gotta stop Danford! We gotta—"

"*You* got to shut up," Bill cut him off sharply. "I got enough to deal with here. I don't need no outraged cavaliers from Philadelphia!"

Bill raised his voice again to be heard above.

"Danford?"

"Yo!"

"We can bargain without the torture sessions! Just leave the women out of it and deal man to man."

"*Shove* your man to man, Hickok! I'll deal any goddamn way I want to, and you'll eat it and you'll *like* it, you puffed-up gal-boy!"

"So start dealing, mouth. What's your terms?"

"Simple. We're riding out, and you're letting us go. First you back off the slope so we can leave. Each one of us will have a woman close by on a lead line. The first time you get cute, the bitches get aired out. Those terms jake by you?"

When Bill hesitated, Danford added, "You wanna hear that cow bellow again?"

"The terms are acceptable," Bill shouted back. "We're moving back. But draw back away from the opening first. No free shots."

"Rot in hell!" Danford shouted. But he did move back.

"Scuttle backwards quick when I give the word," Bill ordered Josh. "But keep your eyes on that opening when you're exposed. If they try to cold-deck us, flatten into the ground. It's a rough angle for an easy bead—they'll have to waste lead."

However, the two men made it to the bottom of the slope without incident.

"Run fetch the horses," Bill told Josh. "We won't follow right off, but I want to be ready."

However, both men were suddenly caught off guard by events up above.

Evidently Danford didn't trust Hickok's word. Danford, Coyote, and their captives, along with several extra horses, suddenly emerged from the hidden cavern and began escaping down the slope.

"Damn fools," Bill muttered. "They're going too fast on that shale."

Bill made no move to intervene, knowing neither Danford nor the twisted Coyote would hesitate to kill the women. Josh could see how each woman's horse was side-lined to the men's saddle horns by a short rope, controlling them.

But Bill was right, and the inevitable came to pass. One of the big bays carrying a woman—Josh had no idea which one yet—suddenly stumbled hard on loose shale, front legs splaying out from under it.

The man holding the horse had no choice but to let go of the line or risk tripping his own horse. Josh, his heart leaping into his throat, watched the woman land hard on the slope and then start rolling and tumbling toward the bottom, not far from where he and Bill stood.

Yuma Bustout

"God kiss me!" Bill exclaimed.

The tumble was hard but fast, and within seconds the unfortunate woman had drawn up at the base of the slope. She lay ominously still.

Bill raced off toward her on foot at the same time the rider decided to retrieve his captive. The other escaped convict, Josh saw, was fleeing into the night with his prisoner. But clearly Bill figured all bets were off concerning this other one.

Both men drew closer, and because he was running so hard, Bill left his guns holstered. Josh watched the rider lift his scatter gun and empty both barrels at Wild Bill.

Luckily, the range was a little long for the rock-salt loads to be lethal. But enough of it scraped and cut Bill to make him swerve, then stumble.

He came up cussing, but also fanning his hammer, blood streaming into his eyes from the rock-salt cuts.

Luckily for the horseman, Bill was still disoriented, and his shots flew inches wide. The rider cursed, then suddenly gave up his quest. He whirled his horse and raced to catch up with his companion.

"Is she still alive, Bill?" Josh shouted, running to join Hickok where he knelt over the supine woman.

Josh looked over Bill's shoulder, then forgot to take his next breath—the young woman lying there in the silver moonlight was so pretty, she took it away. He recognized her instantly as the immensely popular tragedian.

"Is she breathing?" Josh said, almost whispering in his reverence. "She ain't dead, is she?"

"If she is," Bill answered calmly enough, his theatrical words amazing Josh, "then 'death lies on her lips like an untimely frost on the fairest flower in all the fields.'"

Josh blinked stupidly. "Huh?"

"You're slipping, kid. That line's from *Romeo and Juliet*. Well, good. She's still breathing, and her pulse is strong. C'mon, quit gawking at her and give me a hand, moon calf! We've gotta get her sheltered before our friends decide to come back."

Chapter Eleven

"'Preciate it, kid," Bill said when Josh finished cleaning the worst of his rock-salt wounds with clean cistern water. "Now come on outside and give me a hand."

With Connie hurt and badly shaken from her fall, the trio had little choice but to take over the newly deserted shelter hidden under the rock shelf—called Devil's Shelf on Bill's Army field map.

Bill coaxed the distraught and agitated woman into downing the last of the Old Taylor in his flask. Not used to spirits, the exhausted actress had quickly fallen asleep near the glowing fire pit, comfortable on Bill and Josh's combined bedrolls.

The two men went through the saddle pockets of the horse she rode. They made short work of some jerked beef and hardtack they found.

While they ate, Bill carefully studied the long slope

in the moonlight, searching for any movements or shapes that didn't fit. Satisfied it was safe, he led Josh out from under the overhang.

"Grab his legs, wouldja?" Bill nodded at the sprawled body of Lorenzo. "We leave him right here, we're just inviting predators into the cave."

Taking their time about it—for it was a big body and both men were bone-tired—they dragged Lorenzo off to one side of the slope, well away from the vulnerable rock chamber.

"I'm damned if I'll bury any man tried to kill me," Bill remarked as they walked back to the shelter. "Besides, we won't be here long enough to worry about the stink."

"You think Miss Emmerick's hurt bad?" Josh asked.

Bill shook his head, peeling back the wrapper of a cheroot. "Twisted ankle, some cuts and bruises, got some scrapes. Say, kid? Why'n't you go up there and give her a thorough physical examination, huh?"

"That ain't funny," Josh protested.

"No, not funny. Just fun. Anyhow, I'll wager that fall didn't knock the sheer, spiteful cussedness outta her."

They didn't have to wait long to find out—Connie was wide awake when they returned. She sat on one of the bedrolls, trying to comb a snag out of her hair. The flickering orange light of the chamber turned the big bruise on her chin into a flattering beauty mark.

"Miss Emmerick!" Josh exclaimed, practically tripping over his own feet as he hurried in to pour her a cup of coffee. "My name is Joshua Robinson, at your service. I'm a reporter for the *New York Herald*. May I add, ma'am, that I am a devoted follower of your art, and—"

"Mr. Hickok?" Connie cut Josh off as if he were an irksome Bible-thumper on the street. She sounded furious. "Mr. Hickok, I presume you must be the chief authority here?"

Hickok bowed slightly. "Someone must be, madam."

"Of course, but you've let me sleep for *three hours*!"

Bill smote his forehead. "I thought the maid would wake you."

"It's not funny except perhaps to a boor! My sister Anne is with those . . . those monsters! You just let them ride away with her!"

"Now, remember," Bill tried to reason with her, "it ain't like they asked my permission to take her."

"But they're even more desperate now! She doesn't stand a chance. We can't waste time!"

"She does too have a chance, though slim. And we're not wasting time. It just seems that way to you."

Bill said this almost absently, for he was distracted by the smooth, white roundness of her left shoulder, exposed by her torn dress.

"Kid?"

"Yeah?"

It cost Bill an effort to tug his eyes away from the trail-weathered but still beautiful woman.

"Kid, you figure you could escort Miss Emmerick back across the border into Arizona?"

Josh couldn't believe his ears. Jeez! Could a hungry bear eat honey?

"Sure I could," the kid replied, a bit too eagerly.

Bill snorted. "Stout lad. You should have easy riding if you travel after dark and take plenty of this water with you."

"What about my sister?" Connie demanded.

"Like you said," Bill told her. "She hasn't got much time. So I'm going after her now."

"Yes, well, fine. But . . . alone?"

"Why not? That's how I usually operate," Bill assured her.

"Yes, I've read that about Wild Bill Hickok. But tell me, this young man here . . ."

Connie abruptly turned to look at Josh. She appraised him so frankly that he blushed.

"Would he be more useful to you," she asked Bill, "if he stayed here in Mexico? Never mind me."

Bill, too, looked at the kid, smoothing his mustache with one finger.

"Well, he's a city boy and reads Sir Walter Scott, God help us all. But I've discovered he's a good man to have along."

"Then he stays," Connie announced as if she were the obvious boss here. "And I stay. I sha'n't return to the U.S. until Anne is safe!"

Josh saw a grin tugging at Bill's lips.

"You sha'n't, huh?" Hickok asked her. "All due respect, Miss Emmerick. But that decision isn't yours to make."

Connie's nostrils flared, and she started to protest. But the emotional hell she'd endured in the past few days now exacted its toll: She suddenly burst into tears.

Josh wrung his hands like a helpless midwife.

"Aww, *please* don't cry, Miss Emmerick," Josh said

awkwardly. He looked a plea at Hickok. "Maybe Bill will change his mind about us going."

"Don't let her tears dupe you," Bill said, though his tone was playful. "This young woman isn't your ordinary, run-of-the-mill actress. She's trained to cry right on cue."

Bill was mostly teasing, and despite her distraught state, Connie realized this. She actually smiled briefly through her tears.

"For a rough frontier fellow," she told Bill, impressed, "you seem to know something about the theater."

"Well, let's see. I know that you threw me out of one."

She looked surprised, drying her tears with a fold of her dress. "I? When and where?"

"Umm, back in summer of '70. In Frisco."

Connie actually blushed. "Yes, I remember! But . . . that man was you?"

He nodded. "I look different in a topper and swallow tails."

"Well, you might have sent in your card. And I'm always somewhat . . . aloof after an exhaustive performance, Mr. Hickok."

"Please call me Bill."

"At any rate, you didn't *have* to leave so meekly, Mr. Hick—Bill."

Hickok's eyes took her measure. "I'll remember you told me that."

She flushed again. "Well, of course, I'm engaged now," she hastened to qualify.

"I'll still remember it," Bill assured her. "Jim Paxton's range is big, but it doesn't include a man's thoughts. Now, get ready to ride. You insist on staying, so we're all three going after your sister."

Even in the vast Sonora country, it took no time at all for important news to spread. Soon it was widely known that the famous American *actriz* was now with Wild Bill Hickok.

Jim Paxton, his worst fears confirmed, refused to allow a newspaper into his home. In public, he expressed heartfelt statements of support for Hickok and his fiancée; privately, however, he succumbed to his jealous rage. He was a national laughingstock! It would be one cold day in hell before he turned his good name and fortune over to Hickok's conquests.

Border troubleshooter Butch Jeffries learned the news about Hickok and Connie while en route to a remote Mexican Army observation post called Eagle Rock. It was a squalid collection of tents and cassions crowding the unmarked border with the Arizona Territory.

The OP was commanded by Lieutenant Pablo Gonzales, a veteran combat officer sharpened by years of fighting the wily Apaches. Butch Jeffries knew how poorly Mexican soldiers were paid, so over the years he and Gonzales had struck several "mutually beneficial" arrangements.

"Personally," Butch said, "I like Hickok. I played five-card with him once in El Paso. A real gentleman. He's got style, real style."

Gonzales had a solid jaw, a thin mustache, and coffee-colored eyes that could trap a man like lance points. His English was rough at times, but better than Butch's Spanish.

Yuma Bustout

"So much 'style,' eh, *'mano*, that you will gladly help me kill him?"

The two men sat under the fly of Gonzales's tent, sharing the little rectangle of shade. Behind them, two squads of bored soldiers had met to do battle—not with weapons but with red and black ants. One man ran around recording bets before the ants were turned loose on each other.

"But I'm *not* trying to kill him," Butch objected. "I've been hired to kill the woman with him. So I'm offering up Hickok's hide as payment for killing the woman right along with him."

"Kill her?" Gonzales almost whispered the words, so great was his surprise. "But who could want such a beauty dead?"

Butch shrugged apologetically. "Now, now, Pablo. You know a businessman's agent must practice discretion."

Gonzales considered this startling proposition. He did not exactly trust Jeffries or any gringo. But trust was never an issue between such men as they, for no man expected to receive what he refused to give.

Still—this steel-eyed, polite American had never lied to him where an illegal dollar or peso was involved.

"I just heard the woman is with Hickok," Gonzales finally said. "And of course I have heard these *rumores* about a reward for Hickok. So you claim it is true?"

"May I rot in hell if it's not. You can cash Hickok's head in for ten thousand *yanqui* greenbacks. Just a short trip into Texas. There's a rich, grieving father there waiting for it—Hickok killed his boy up north in Abilene, Kansas."

Up north? Kansas might as well have been the

Judd Cole

North Pole, so far as Gonzales cared. But a trip into Texas could certainly be managed for so much money, *por Dios!*

As for Jeffries—Jim Paxton only said he wanted his fiancé killed. He never stipulated exactly who must do it or precisely how it get done.

"This woman," Gonzales said, pulling thoughtfully at his chin. "This *bonita actriz*, Connie Emmer—however one says it. I hear she is a feast for a man's eyes, true?"

"Blond hair the color of new wheat," Butch goaded. "White skin like the finest lotion. And more curves than a man can brake for."

"And tell me, amigo. *Must* she be killed—right away, I mean?"

Butch grinned, catching the officer's drift.

"Well, eventually she must be killed. What a man did with her beforehand, of course, would be his own affair."

Gonzales matched his grin. "Of course. The Code of Chivalry leaves a man much privacy."

"As for killing Hickok, I'd never try it alone," Jeffries freely admitted. "That's why I'm dealing you in. You could take your ten best men. Catch Hickok in the open desert with those bloodthirsty devils of yours, he'd be buzzard bait."

"So you say."

"So I *know*. Then you simply pay each man fifty dollars American, leaves you ninety-five hundred dollars. In a country where tequila is only fifty cents a bottle, where twenty dollars buys a top horse. *Qué dices, viejo?* What say, old boy?"

Gonzales let his gaze drift toward his men, in a ring on their knees, cheering on their favorite insects.

Yuma Bustout

They were bored to the point of insanity—this was the worst duty in the Mexican military. It would be easy to find ten volunteers for this lucrative venture.

Especially with the extra incentive a beautiful woman promised.

"I will certainly do it," Gonzales replied. "But it is Hickok my men will kill first. The woman will not be wasted. Not out here."

"Fine by me, as long as you kill her when you're done with her. She must not escape."

Gonzales smiled at that thought. "We always kill them when we're done, *'mano*. Stone them into silence, you see, and then there is no crime, true?"

Chapter Twelve

Since their enemy's trail looped back past La Cola, Bill delayed long enough to check the hiding place inside the knoll south of town. The moment Connie told him and Josh about the silver, Bill had predicted it would be gone when they got to the spot. Bill's prediction panned out.

For two days Hickok's little group dogged their enemy's trail steadily east by southeast. But like Danford's bunch, they were forced to ride after dark only. By now soldiers, freebooters, ragtag "armies of the people," and numerous gangs of highway bandits were on the prowl for the two famous intruders from el Norte. Indians, too, were less of a threat after dark.

Not all were bent on murder, of course. But Hickok told Josh tersely that there was no time to sort them all out. Best to just avoid them all.

"They're already halfway across Chihuahua State,"

Bill said as they made camp one morning at dawn, getting ready to hole up for the daylight hours. "My guess is they mean to stay more or less on a straight line toward New Orleans. San Antonio would be closer, but New Orleans has plenty of banks that take gold and silver in quantity routinely."

Josh was listening. But he also kept his eyes on Connie, worried about her. So was Bill, though he wouldn't let on. She refused to complain, especially after making such a fuss about going with them.

But clearly Constance Emmerick was suffering. The unrelenting sun and heat allowed a person no more than an hour or two of sleep, and then only if snatched before noon. The meager diet and scanty water rations—plus the constant fear that Anne's body would turn up around the next turn of the trail—exacted a harsh toll on her artistic constitution.

Yet both men greatly admired her pluck and will and determination. "A woman who speaks four languages and reads Plato," Bill had remarked to Josh at one point. "And after all she's been through, to take more of this. She's some pumpkins, all right."

They'd set up camp in a low wash where boulders threw some shade for them and the horses. Josh had the first watch. Before Bill turned in, he studied his map again.

"I think I got a fix on their route now," he told Josh. "They'll cross into the States just south of the Texas Big Bend country—at Piedras Negras or maybe Del Rio. Then they'll stick close to the Gulf of Mexico, because the U.S. hardly patrols that far down. They'll follow the coast of Texas and Louisiana to New Orleans."

Yuma Bustout

Connie lay nearby on Josh's bedroll, listening but too tired to comment.

"The thing of it is," Bill mused, "they know damn well they can't afford to be tailed all that way."

"Meaning," Josh supplied, "that they're pretty confident they're going to kill us?"

Bill nodded, glancing toward Connie again. "I don't like this, kid. Maybe you better take her across the border to safety after all."

Connie sat up. "I heard that. Never mind me, please. If having Joshua with you increases Anne's chances even one whit, then I want him here."

"Fair enough," Bill told her. "Now, get some sleep."

Bill, too, stretched out in his blanket, trying to rest before the day's heat struck triple digits. It seemed he was just starting to tumble over the threshold of sleep when Josh shook him roughly awake.

"My watch already?" Bill grumbled, thumbing the sleep from his eyes.

"No, trouble coming," Josh informed him. "Look!"

He pointed toward the northwest. Bill, guessing from the sun that it was still forenoon, followed Josh's finger. Out on the shimmering horizon, a formation of riders approached in a staggered echelon.

"Soldiers," Bill said immediately, for he could see the tall shako hats and plumes even from here. "Mexican regulars."

"Think they've seen us from that far?" Josh wondered. "This wash is kinda low. We should be below the horizon for them."

"We are, you young fool," Bill groused. "But lookit your pony! I told you to use hobbles, not tether it.

He's wandered up to the high ground, and they've spotted him."

"What is it?" Connie demanded, for she was already awake when Bill got up.

"Federales," Bill told her. "Maybe ten, a dozen of them. Bearing right down on us. We can dig sand wallows and fight, or we can hightail it, maybe find better ground."

"Could we hold them off here?" Josh asked. "They have to cross open ground to close in on us."

"True," Bill said. "But what if they're well provisioned? We've got no food and next to no water. They decide to, they could just ring us in and wait it out, starve us."

"Yeah," Josh said. "I didn't think about that."

Bill slid both guns out of their holsters, checking his loads.

"Both of you," he said. "Saddle up. Looks to me like their horses are tired. Let's see if we can outrun them."

Lieutenant Gonzales, armed with good tips from Butch Jeffries, had ridden out of the garrison at Eagle Rock almost eighteen hours earlier.

He had selected ten men known for their steady aim and their combat courage. For the sake of speed, he ordered each man to bring only his blanket roll, his carbine, thirty rounds of ammo, and enough rations for a week in the field.

Bearing east by southeast, they left Sonora, crossed the Continental Divide, and entered the neighboring Mexican state of Chihuahua.

Despite the hard conditions, the men appreciated this break in the routine of garrison life. And a

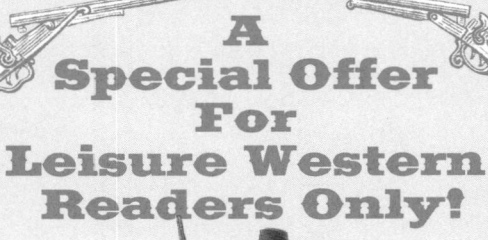

A Special Offer For Leisure Western Readers Only!

Get FOUR FREE* Western Novels

Travel to the Old West in all its glory and drama—without leaving your home!

Plus, you'll save between $3.00 and $6.00 every time you buy!

EXPERIENCE THE ADVENTURE AND THE DRAMA OF THE OLD WEST WITH THE GREATEST WESTERNS ON THE MARKET TODAY... FROM LEISURE BOOKS

As a home subsriber to the Leisure Western Book Club, you'll enjoy the most exciting new voices of the Old West, plus classic works by the masters in new paperback editions. Every month Leisure Books brings you the best in Western fiction, from Spur-Award-winning, quality authors. Upcoming book club releases include new-to-paperback novels by such great writers as:

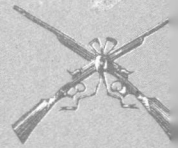

Max Brand   Robert J. Conley   Gary McCarthy   Judy Alter
Frank Roderus   Douglas Savage   G. Clifton Wisler
David Robbins   Douglas Hirt

as well as long out-of-print classics by legendary authors like:

Will Henry   T.V. Olsen   Gordon D. Shirreffs

Each Leisure Western breaths life into the cowboys, the gunfighters, the homesteaders, the mountain men and the Indians who fought to survive in the vast frontier. Discover for yourself the excitement, the power and the beauty that have been enthralling readers each and every month.

SAVE BETWEEN $3.00 AND $6.00 EACH TIME YOU BUY!

Each month, the Leisure Western Book Club brings you four terrific titles from Leisure Books, America's leading publisher of Western fiction. EACH PACKAGE WILL SAVE YOU BETWEEN $3.00 AND $6.00 FROM THE BOOKSTORE PRICE! And you'll never miss a new title with our convenient home delivery service.

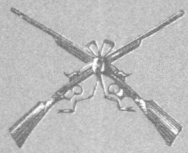

Here's how it works. Each package will carry a FREE* 10-DAY EXAMINATION privilege. At the end of that time, if you decide to keep your books, simply pay the low invoice price of $13.44, ($14.50 US in Canada) no shipping or handling charges added.* HOME DELIVERY IS ALWAYS FREE*. With this price it's like getting one book free every month.

AND YOUR FIRST FOUR-BOOK SHIPMENT IS TOTALLY FREE*! IT'S A BARGAIN YOU CAN'T BEAT!

LEISURE BOOKS   A Division of Dorchester Publishing Co., Inc.

GET YOUR 4 FREE* BOOKS NOW— A VALUE BETWEEN $16 AND $20

Mail the Free* Book Certificate Today!

FREE* BOOKS CERTIFICATE!

YES! I want to subscribe to the Leisure Western Book Club. Please send me my 4 FREE* BOOKS. Then, each month, I'll receive the four newest Leisure Western Selections to preview FREE* for 10 days. If I decide to keep them, I will pay the Special Member's Only discounted price of just $3.36 each, a total of $13.44 ($14.50 US in Canada). This saves me between $3 and $6 off the bookstore price. There are no shipping, handling or other charges.* There is no minimum number of books I must buy and I may cancel the program at any time. In any case, the 4 FREE* BOOKS are mine to keep—at a value of between $17 and $20!

*In Canada, add $5.00 Canadian shipping and handling per order for first shipment. For all subsequent shipments to Canada the cost of membership in the Book Club is $14.50 US, which includes $7.50 shipping and handling per month. All payments must be made in US currency.

Name _____

Address _____

City _____ State_____ Country_____

Zip _____ Telephone _____

If under 18, parent or guardian must sign. Terms, prices and conditions subject to change. Subscription subject to acceptance. Leisure Books reserves the right to reject any order or cancel any subscription.

Get Four Books Totally FREE* — A Value between $16 and $20

Tear here and mail your FREE* book card today!

PLEASE RUSH MY FOUR FREE* BOOKS TO ME RIGHT AWAY!

LeisureWestern Book Club
P.O. Box 6613
Edison, NJ 08818-6613

AFFIX STAMP HERE

chance to kill the *famoso* Bill Hickok was anything but routine. Especially since the lieutenant promised a cash bonus for each man, assuming Hickok was sent under.

They had spotted the lone horse perhaps thirty minutes ago—a black-and-white piebald with a roached mane, the very same horse Jeffries described. It belonged to the fresh-scrubbed youth riding with Wild Bill Hickok.

"Teniente!" called out a lance corporal riding to the right of Gonzales. "They have spotted us! They are running!"

The formation had been approaching at a canter to preserve the horses. Now Gonzales raised his right fist high in the air and pumped it up and down—the signal to kick their horses to a full gallop.

The pursuit was on.

Bill had told Josh once that the most important quality of any horse was not apparent in its color or markings. It was a quality the Spanish called *brio escondido*, the hidden vigor.

Bill's roan, like Josh's Sioux-trained piebald, could draw on deep reserves of strength and wind—especially since the nostrils of both animals had been slit to increase their wind.

Connie's big combination horse, in contrast, soon began to blow foam and lose speed.

Bill cursed their luck, but he could have predicted it. The big, seventeen-hand "American" horses were strong enough, all right, and could be sharply trained. But although big and pretty, they lacked any real bottom in a life-and-death chase like this one.

As Connie's mount began to flounder, Josh and Bill

slowed to keep her between them. Gradually, the pursuing force closed the gap.

Josh glanced over his shoulder and saw gun muzzles spit puffs of smoke. The range was still too long, and the bullets struck wide or short, kicking up geysers of sand. But the Mexican soldiers, veterans of such fighting, only used misses to improve their aim.

Soon, bullets whanged in so close by that it was getting dangerous. Bill tugged his Winchester from the boot and twisted around at a gallop, throwing the weapon into his shoulder.

He got two rounds off quickly, then cursed when a spent cartridge jammed in the ejection port. The unrelenting desert sun had heat-warped the brass casings. There was no way Bill could clear it while riding this fast.

Desperate now, he scoured the terrain for a place to hole up and fight a defensive stand. But the stretch of desert between here and Old El Paso, about fifty miles due east according to his map, was one of the flattest and barest in all of northern Mexico.

Connie's horse stumbled, sides heaving. The *federales* were now close enough that the fleeing trio could hear their horses snorting and their bit rings chinking.

A Mexican fired his rifle, and a bullet thwapped into Bill's saddle fender.

"That's it!" he shouted to Josh. "We can't outrun 'em!"

Josh goggled at him. "You mean . . . we surrender?"

"You loco?" Bill demanded. "These boys ain't planning on taking no prisoners—'cept maybe one," Bill added in a lower voice, looking at Connie. "And she'll be killed when they finish with her."

Yuma Bustout

More rounds whistled and hummed past their ears, one punching into Josh's hat.

"Keep riding!" Bill ordered his two companions. The next moment, both ivory-gripped Colts were in his fists, the reins in his teeth, and Hickok had wheeled around to attack the attackers.

The move may have looked like pure suicide to the soldiers. But Hickok was counting on both his horse and his legendary skill with pistols.

For perhaps five seconds, the Mexicans were too surprised to do anything at all except keep charging. But as Bill hurtled closer, they sent a withering cloud of lead at him.

Fire-away knew what to do even without Bill's goading. The battle-savvy horse began running an avoidance pattern, bucking and dodging. With bullets fanning his long curls and screaming in his ears, Bill opened up with the Peacemaker in his right fist. Six quick shots.

The range was long for a short gun, and Bill was firing *at* moving targets *from* a moving target. Nonetheless, he had the distinct satisfaction of watching three men tumble from the saddle. The foot of one got caught in the stirrup; his horse continued forward, the body bouncing wildly beside it.

But Bill had no time to count his coups. With the line still advancing, he opened up with his remaining gun. Two more men flew from the saddle—including the officer in charge.

That broke the will of the attackers. Even as Bill wheeled Fire-away and raced to join his fleeing companions, the Mexican soldiers lost their tight formation and became a bunch of confused, milling individuals with no one in charge.

Judd Cole

* * *

"God Almighty," Butch Jeffries said softly as he lowered his field glasses.

The frontier veteran felt badly shaken by what he had just seen. He knew that Hickok was a formidable foe. But holy mother of God! The man had singlehandedly wiped out half a squad of soldiers—and with a short gun, at that!

Jeffries had been trailing Gonzales at a safe distance since the Mexican had set out yesterday. He had wanted to verify, with his own eyes, that the Connie Emmerick problem had been eliminated.

Instead, he had found out why Hickok was a hero even in Paris and London. It didn't matter how many lies were told about Wild Bill—the truth was enough to stagger the imagination. Jeffries had just witnessed that.

What he saw only deepened his respect for Hickok. But of course, it did not change what Butch had to do. Obviously, killing Connie Emmerick was going to be harder than he—or Jim Paxton—could have known.

However, Butch had accepted Paxton's terms and he still meant to get it done. Clearly, though, a man would have to work around Hickok to carry it through.

Fortunately, Jeffries reminded himself as he returned to his horse, this border country held many advantages for a man who knew it well. Hickok had won this battle, but the longer war would sink him.

Chapter Thirteen

"Damn good thing we got enough horses," Danford remarked as he heaved a heavy pack saddle to the ground. "This stuff ain't so heavy when it's spread around."

Coyote slid one of the gleaming silver bars out and studied it in the sunlight.

"Oh, we'll spread it around, all right," the breed said in his flat voice. "Two shares 'steada four. I didn't cotton to them Hanchon boys."

Coyote made a point of meeting Anne's eyes before he added, "Leaves more for us, boss. More of everything."

Coyote slid the metal knife from his boot—the same cheap but effective weapon that had killed one prison guard and castrated another. He laughed with a boy's pleasure in mischief when the frightened woman went a shade paler.

Judd Cole

"Stop that," Danford told him mildly.

"Don't like it when an Injun rowels a white woman?" Coyote goaded him.

Danford, however, was preoccupied with other problems and just shook this remark off like it was a fly in his face.

"Listen," he said, "I don't miss the Hanchon boys either. Both of 'em was whiners and they stunk like an outhouse. But they was handy boys in a scrap. With Hickok on our drag, I'd rather have the extra guns. Here you go, Missus Gov."

Danford, smirking a bit because he didn't like being polite, handed Anne a spoon and a tin can of peaches he'd just opened. Earlier, he and Coyote had tied Anne up long enough to ambush a southbound coach headed for Villa Ahumada.

Between the driver, the guard they killed, and four frightened passengers, the two had made a good haul. It included tinned fruit, liquor, and sandwiches.

Now Danford, Coyote, and their prisoner were resting in a welcome stretch of river valley near the Mexican border town of Piedras Negras. There was good graze here, and ample shade from cottonwoods. They stripped their horses of their rigging and led them down to the Rio Grande to drink their fill.

Anne was ashamed of herself for eating these peaches like some starving street urchin, slurping them out of the can as the men were doing. But she was famished, and this was the first truly edible food she'd tasted since being abducted. Damn these monsters to hell, anyway!

Oh, thank God for men like Wild Bill Hickok, she thought yet again. No, he hadn't rescued her as he had Connie. But it was his persistence—and his reputation—that had these two filthy beasts on edge constantly. Worried, looking over their shoulders, starting at the least noise and drawing their weapons, only to smile foolishly and put them away again.

Scared men had little luxury for lust. And so far she had not been raped. So far.

Coyote's voice cut into her thoughts.

"How'd you know about this place?" he asked Danford.

Coyote meant the low storage shed built beside a crumbling dock near the river. It was obviously long deserted, judging from the sagging doors and all the birds that flitted in and out of the building.

"I ran a smuggling ring here for the Rebs during the war, that's how," Fargo boasted.

He paused to eliminate half of a roast-beef sandwich in one bite. Then, talking with his mouth full, he added:

"This part of Texas grew cotton. When the Yankees seized the southern ports, we started shipping bales down the Rio to Matamoros. I figured the place might still be here."

Danford placed one hand on a taut canvas pack beside him. It was perhaps the size of a big clasp Bible. Danford considered it the best find of all when they robbed that coach.

"This place'll be perfect," he insisted. "I can have it set up in less than an hour. Then all we gotta do is hide down by the river and wait for Hickok."

Both men looked at Anne, who had suddenly lost her appetite as she realized what that canvas pack was. Now she understood their plan, and it sent spikes of cold fear into her limbs.

Judd Cole

"S'matter, sugar-britches?" Coyote goaded her. "Us convicts play too rough for a high-toned society bitch like you?"

Anne tried to shame him by meeting his eyes. But that only made her nauseous after a few seconds.

Danford gingerly unsnapped a flap on one side of the pack. It was marked clearly in English, and now Anne could read it: DANGER! HANDLE CAREFULLY! HIGHLY EXPLOSIVE! The invoice with it showed the stagecoach had been delivering it special order from Albuquerque to a railroad construction company near Chihuahua.

"I know this stuff," Danford said. "Even used it once to blow a bank vault in Gallup, New Mexico—though I used too much and blew half the town away. It's partially stabilized nitroglycerin in a wax base."

Coyote frowned. "But how we gonna detonate it? Don't we have to light a fuse? Hell, Hickok ain't deaf."

"You're behind times," Danford assured him. "New inventions every day. We got this with it."

He slid a coil of copper wire and a little handheld spark generator out of the pack.

"A galvanic detonator," he explained. "See that little cap well on top the explosive? We just jam the end of the wire in there along with some primer charge. We can hide way the hell down by the river. Just close this little switch after he goes in the house. No noise, and instant detonation."

"My sister," Anne said. "She might go in too."

"Helluva waste," Coyote said.

"She's so young," Anne protested. "She's so talented and—"

"Put away your violin," Danford snapped. "Nobody

wants to hurt your precious sister. Hickok ain't no greenhorn! You think he ain't going to clear that building first before he lets Connie go in? Use some goddamn sense."

"'Sense,'" Anne repeated woodenly. "What do either of you insane monsters know about *sense*?"

As Bill had predicted, Danford and Coyote were bearing toward the Mexican town of Piedras Negras. Every border rat on the dodge knew that area was seldom patrolled by American soldiers. The way the Army saw it, anyone foolish enough to be out in that scalding inferno could cross at will.

Edible game was scarce. But Bill was able to snag several plump rattlesnakes during the night rides. Connie, who had chosen hunger over colt meat, promptly pronounced snake meat of gourmet quality.

Once, during a brief break, she surprised both men by setting her troubles aside for a moment.

"Bill?" she asked.

"Mmm?"

"You always call Joshua 'kid' or Longfellow. Don't you ever call people by their first names?"

"What kind of foolish question is that?"

"I don't know," she told him defiantly. "But Joshua is *not* a kid."

"Hell, I know that. The kid saved my life once."

"See? You just did it! Call me Connie, I dare you!"

"Connie," he spat out defiantly, and she and Josh both laughed at the obvious discomfort in his face.

Only a few hours after this exchange, they had reached a clutch of rocks concealing a little seep spring. Since day was coming on, Bill called a halt to sleep. Because visibility was clear in all directions, and Connie reliable, she was allowed to take a stint on guard so both exhausted men could sleep.

They both soon discovered why she wanted them both asleep. Josh, tugged out of fitful rest by some faint noise, rolled over in his blanket, then came wide awake, heart pounding.

The rocks surrounding the seep spring only partially concealed it from view. And now Josh saw Connie standing in water up to her knees, naked, wringing out her wet hair.

Josh turned to look toward Bill's bedroll. Hickok, too, was wide awake and watching.

"She coulda been quieter," he whispered to Josh, winking. "Her fault if we got a free show."

"Bill?"

"Yeah?"

"Do you think Danford and them . . . you know? With the women, I mean?"

"What, raped them?"

"Yeah," Josh said.

"Not Connie, I don't think. She's not got that look in her eye like some proud women get afterward—that kill glint. But Anne Jacobs?"

Bill took one last appreciative glance at the sylvan bather. Then he rolled over.

"Anne Jacobs," Josh heard him say, "is in one world of hurt. Rape ain't her biggest danger. Get some sleep, kid. You'll be needing it."

The trio pushed on after dark, making good time as they approached the border. Danford and Coyote were making no attempt to cover their trail.

By now Josh had learned, from watching Bill, how

to cut sign. But in this generous moonwash, it wasn't even necessary to dismount to spot the trail. Especially with heavily laden packhorses leaving deep prints with their hind hooves.

About an hour before dawn, they crested a low hill above the Rio Grande Valley.

Bill pointed upriver. About a mile west, a few lights winked in the blue-black morning dimness on the Mexican side of the border.

"Piedras Negras," he said. "But their trail veers right. They avoided town."

Bill swung down out of the saddle and knelt over a clump of horse manure. He broke it open with the toe of his boot.

"Less than twelve hours since they passed this way," he announced, judging by the dryness of the droppings. "But they've been riding hard for days now. And more tough sledding when they cross. So the question is—are they camped nearby, resting up and laying a trap for us?"

Josh glanced around in the cool morning mist, a shiver moving down his spine.

"Connie," Bill said, making a point of stressing her first name, so that she smiled at him. "Move up in the middle when we ride out. Kid, take up the drag, I'll ride point. With all these trees and bushes, we're riding into good ambush country again."

"Least we'll be in Texas soon," Josh remarked as they moved out again. "Can we ride in daylight then?"

Bill nodded. "But worry about Texas when we get there, kid. Right now we're still in Mexico, and we might play hell getting out of here. Don't forget, the last thing Danford and Coyote want is to be followed in the States. They know we can use the telegraph against them."

While they rode, moving closer and closer to the river as they descended the slope of the valley, the eastern sky began to lighten. Perhaps thirty minutes before sunrise, they rode up out of a deep cutbank, and Bill suddenly halted them.

He waved Josh up. When the kid reached him, Bill pointed ahead through a cottonwood grove.

About three hundred yards ahead, Josh could see the wide, shallow Rio Grande, reflecting bright diamonds of moonlight. A low building stood beside it. Down by the river, a knot of horses were tethered.

"That answers one of my questions," Bill told Josh. "They're still in Mexico. I recognize those animals. But the big question is whether or not we've caught them out or this is just an ambush."

"If it's a trap," Josh said, "would they expose their horses like that? We could kill those animals right now, and they'd be out of business."

Bill sent the kid an appreciative glance. "You're starting to think like a trailsman, Longfellow. That's a tempting idea. I could shoot them from here with the rifle."

Bill went so far as to slide the Winchester from its boot. But then his face settled into a frown as he studied the house some more.

"If it is a trap, meant to lure us down, then killing the horses is our best play," Bill said, thinking out loud. "But what if it isn't a trap? That means I'm warning them inside the building. Waking them up so they can fight. And maybe—"

Bill cut himself off before he said it, for Connie had

ridden up to join them. But she finished for him. "And maybe they'll kill Anne if you wake them?"

Bill nodded. "The thing of it is, we've made good time. Probably better time than Danford expected. It makes good sense that they'd rest here before heading into Texas. Especially if they just take turns on sentry."

Bill debated it some more while the first birds began to celebrate dawn.

"I'm going down there," he finally decided. "You two wait right here until I give the hail. If trouble breaks out, kid, stick with Connie. Anything happens to me, you'll be responsible for getting her back to Yuma."

Chapter Fourteen

Hickok leapfrogged from tree to tree, making his way gradually down the slope toward the old shed by the river. He was fully aware that a sentry could be hiding anywhere nearby. So Bill moved quickly when he was exposed, then studied the area thoroughly each time he reached new cover. It was a windy morning, which helped Bill cover his noise.

For a moment he was tempted to check on the horses, see how much grass they'd cut since being bunched near the river. That might give him some idea how long Danford and Coyote had been here.

But Bill nixed that plan. There was too much open ground between him and the horses, and by now it was too light—a bright yellow ball of new sun had pushed itself partway above the eastern horizon. Already, the morning mist was burning off the river.

Closer, ever closer Bill pressed, convinced by now

there was no sentry on duty outside. But that didn't preclude one's hiding in the shadow just inside the open shed door.

A Colt filled Bill's right hand. He kept his ears attuned to warning sounds—any disruption in the murmur of the river or the morning chatter of birds.

By now Bill was only a stone's throw from the low shed. A storage shed, he told himself with a flush of irritation— long and low with no windows he could peek through.

But weathered slab doors, one falling off its leather hinges, slanted open at opposite ends of the structure. Built just like a varmint trap, Bill couldn't help thinking.

Bill eased the leather thong off his hammer and cocked it. He peered around the rough-barked bole of a cottonwood, giving the entire area one last good look before he approached the building.

All quiet up the slope behind him, where Josh waited with Connie. To his right, the horses still grazed contentedly, ignoring the human intruder. And all seemed still and peaceful along the river behind the shed. Bill watched several red-tailed hawks circling back there, looking for prey.

Crouched low and eyes front, his pulse thudding in his ears, Hickok ran the last thirty yards to the shed. Even as he moved, he remembered an old wartime adage that always came back to him willy-nilly during dangerous moments: *You never hear the shot that kills you.*

Bill fetched up beside the nearest open door and hoped he was still hidden from anyone awake inside. He waited until his breathing had settled a bit. Then, cautious as a cat, he peeked inside.

Yuma Bustout

The first thing he saw was a rectangle of light at the opposite end—the other doorway. At first, however, he could make out little inside the shed, the light was so meager. But a warning prickled his nose: the reek of rotgut whiskey.

A moment later, a tight bubble of elation swelled inside Hickok.

There! He had just spotted the prone shapes of three people sleeping.

Bill couldn't believe the luck of his timing. And he meant to get it done quickly: identify which sleeper was Anne, then plug the other two before they could wake up. Nobody in America wanted Danford or Coyote back alive—not after the trail of bodies they'd left behind, beginning in Arizona.

Bill had a rule concerning the most cold-blooded murderers. He borrowed it from the Mexicans, one of the smartest things they'd invented in his opinion: *Ley Fuga*, or "Flight Law." A fleeing felon could be shot dead. And, of course, for every one shot trying to "escape," the law-abiding citizens saved money on food, lodging, and expensive trials and appeals.

Bill took two steps into the shed when he noticed it through the far door: those red-tailed hawks from earlier. They had circled a spot on the riverbank and started to land. Then, abruptly, they scattered in a panic and flitted off.

It could have been anything that scattered them. But in that moment, Bill realized something else, and it made his flesh crawl against his shirt: three sleepers, evidently, but no snoring?

Bill cast a more critical glance at the prone shapes, and he realized they were all similar in an unnatural way.

In fact, they weren't sleepers at all. They were stuffed blankets!

Hickok wasted not one more moment trying to puzzle it out. Instincts more basic than thought made him leap backward out the door the very moment he saw this was all a trap. He was still in midair, his heart frozen between beats, when the whole damn world exploded around him in an orange-flashing roar.

So this is death? a sinister voice whispered as Bill felt himself being hurled like a toy ball in a giant's hand.

Josh soon became bored by Bill's slow, methodical approach to the shed. This was the part of Bill's work the dime novels always skipped: all the time spent watching, waiting, or just moving into position.

Instead, Josh turned his attention to the beautiful actress at his side. The two of them were waiting for Bill's all clear; they huddled together behind a cluster of blackberry bushes, perhaps halfway down the slope of the fertile river valley.

"You know, he's different than I expected him to be," Connie observed. She was still watching Hickok when she could spot him, which wasn't often.

"Who?"

"Your friend, Bill Hickok, goose!"

"Different? How?"

"For one thing, he's not as conceited as I expected him to be," she confessed. "Believe me, I know some conceited people."

Josh refused to touch that one. Takes one to know one, he thought.

"I don't think he even realizes just how famous he is," Connie mused.

Yuma Bustout

Josh shrugged off a sting of jealousy.

"Oh yeah, he does," he told her before he could stop himself.

Josh might also have told her how Hickok masterfully exploited fame when it came to bedding beauties like herself. But he bit off the rest of his words. Jealous or no, he was Bill's friend. And Josh considered that an honor.

"Look!" Connie exclaimed. She clutched Josh's arm. "He's running up to the shed! Oh, God, *please* let Anne be there and safe!"

"He's inside," Josh said. "And no gunshots! Good. Either it's empty, or—"

Unexpectedly, Hickok appeared again, this time leaping backward from the shed. Then a boom-cracking explosion made Josh flinch and Connie cry out.

Hickok, already airborne before the blast, was lifted even higher on a rolling comber of wind, smoke, and flame. The shed went up in splinters while Hickok flew perhaps thirty feet, landing in a tumble.

"Stay right here!" Josh ordered Connie, clawing his French pinfire revolver from its chamois holster. "If anything happens to me, *don't* show yourself to anybody down there, understand? Wait till dark, then cross into Texas. Follow the river north to Del Rio."

Josh hadn't seen Bill move yet and didn't know if he was dead or alive. He tore off down the slope. He didn't bother to seek cover, for soon it was clear all the action was down by the river.

Evidently Bill must have cleared that building just in time, for now Josh saw that he had not been badly hurt in the blast. Bill leaped nimbly behind a rotting cottonwood log amid a hammering racket of gunfire.

The shooting originated from the bushes beyond the demolished shed, only yards from the river. At least one weapon was a rifle, Josh realized, watching big chunks of the log disintegrate around Hickok.

Bill didn't dare rise up to aim, but Josh watched Hickok expertly "ear aim" his shots by calculation alone, simply lifting his guns clear and shooting without looking.

"I'm not trying to shoot for score," he told Josh when the ashen-faced youth dove for cover beside him. "I might hit Anne. So I'm just holding them there. Say, thought I told you to stay with Connie?"

"She's safe. I thought you got hurt."

"Nah. Just singed my mustache, the bastards."

A round chunked in close, spraying wood chips in Josh's face.

Bill rolled his head toward the horses bunched behind him. "Danford and Coyote made one big miscalculation, kid. They counted on that blast to kill me. Instead, now they're cut off from their horses."

"Yeah, that's right! The horses! Want me to go shoot them?" Josh suggested.

A round whistled past, nicking bark into Josh's ear.

"Too dangerous," Bill told him. "Besides, remember, they've got Anne. We want them desperate, kid, but not hopeless. Desperate men will still bargain. But hopeless men are past all controlling."

Josh soon saw the wisdom of Bill's reasoning.

"Hey! Hickok?" Danford shouted from his hiding spot.

"Hey what?" Bill shouted back.

"Let's talk turkey!"

"Name your terms."

Yuma Bustout

"You want the woman. We want the horses. Am I right?"

"Sisters come as a set," Bill agreed.

"All right, so let's swap, and you'll have your set."

"I'm all ears," Hickok shouted back. "Keep talking."

"The river's wide and shallow here, only knee deep. You and me will do the swap midstream. Just us two. We'll both be unarmed. You bring the horses, I'll bring the governor's woman."

"Where's Coyote during all this?" Bill demanded.

"Same place your man will be—standing in plain view down in the water, unarmed, with his arms raised high. Agreed?"

"Sounds like a perfect trap to me," a nervous Josh told Wild Bill.

"Sure it is, kid. You think those two jaspers ever do anything on the level? But it's time to fish or cut bait. I'm sick of this case."

"All right, Danford!" Bill shouted. "First send Coyote down to the water where I can see him. Then start bringing Mrs. Jacobs out. I'm dropping back now for the horses."

Bill nudged Josh.

"Ground your weapon, Longfellow. And hoof it down to the water. But keep a weather eye out."

Josh felt sweat ooze out from his hatband, but he did as he was told. Coyote, too, rose from cover, hands high, and stepped out into plain view.

Bill slipped downriver to untie the horses, keeping both his enemies in sight. With Bill leading the horses, and Danford leading Anne Jacobs, both men headed out into the water.

Josh waded out into the river until it almost topped

his boots. He was thus in an excellent position to watch subsequent events unfold.

Coyote waited until all parties were about to converge midstream in the slow, muddy river. Then he moved so swiftly that no one even noticed until he had a good jump. In the space of seconds, he had run to shore, retrieved the stolen Army carbine, and brought it up to the offhand position, sighting in on Hickok.

Even before Josh could shout any warning, Wild Bill reacted with the lightning reflexes of a jungle cat.

He tossed the looped reins in his hand over Danford—barely avoiding snagging Anne too—and jerked him forward hard even as Coyote's carbine barked.

Anne screamed, struggling for footing. Danford cried out when the .56-caliber slug smashed into the hard lump of muscle just under his right shoulder, knocking him down.

Bill's main concern now was to save Anne Jacobs, but he saw how Danford had tied her to his wrist with a short length of sisal. Before Bill could cut it, Coyote forced him to cover down with a flurry of whistling slugs.

Bill had no option but to let Danford seize the horses. The longer Hickok stayed close to Anne, the greater the risk that one of Coyote's bullets would hit her. Hickok's perilous gambit had not fully succeeded, but at least Danford was bleeding hard.

Josh, too, turned and ran just as Coyote whirled on him and sent a bullet his way. The reporter saw it now like a page from a war correspondent's sketchbook: Connie racing down the slope toward the action, her face wan with fright and worry. In that moment, *everyone* was running—Connie, Josh, Wild Bill, Danford, and Anne, each in a different direction.

Damn it, they foxed us, Josh thought bitterly. Danford was wounded, and seriously. But now the bad guys had their horses, their silver, and Anne Jacobs.

Bill had warned Josh that it was Coyote he feared most of all. And it was Coyote alone who was standing still now, smiling his contempt. Josh couldn't help but wonder: Had American legend Wild Bill Hickok finally met his match?

Chapter Fifteen

Butch Jeffries had been tailing Hickok and company ever since Wild Bill killed Gonzales and the other Mexican soldiers. Concerning Hickok, Butch was like a wolf tailing a buffalo herd: afraid to openly attack, but patient enough to wait for an opportunity at easy pickings.

Through brass field glasses, and well hidden at the rim of the Rio Grande Valley, he watched the amazing events down below in the river. And while Danford and Coyote fled with Anne Jacobs, Danford pumping blood like a bellows, Butch watched Connie Emmerick run down the slope to join her friends.

Butch made a good study of the pretty woman, wondering if Hickok had topped her yet. How in God's name, he wondered yet again, could Paxton want that beauty dead just because another man might have enjoyed her first?

Hell, so long as Paxton got his turn, what was his gripe? But some men were like that—wouldn't even read a newspaper if somebody else got to it first.

Butch finally lowered his glasses, slid them back into their leather case, and put that back in his saddle pocket. His dappled gray six-year-old was hobbled out of sight in a copse of dogwood trees.

Well, at any rate, Butch told himself as he slid the gray's headstall into place, at least one thing had become clear: He'd have to take care of Connie Emmerick himself. Watching Hickok dispose of Gonzales and those other federals convinced Butch of that.

Sure, Hickok was dangerous, all right. Six sorts of hell, as a matter of fact. But Butch Jeffries prided himself on getting a job done once he took it on. As for Hickok, his clover was deep, but even deep clover thinned out eventually.

Butch swung up and over, wheeling his gray and heading down toward the Rio Grande. He knew damn well Hickok was going after those two hardcases and their prisoner. It was Hickok's way to hang on like a tick. So Jeffries meant to cross the river himself under cover of a bend just south of Piedras Negras.

Normally, he would hesitate to tail Wild Bill Hickok, a man well-versed in covering his own back trail. But clearly Hickok was tired and trail-worn—distracted by the skill and cunning of his prey.

Butch meant to be patient, bide his time, and wait for the right moment to kill Connie Emmerick.

"We're in Maverick County, Texas, now," Bill informed his companions. "Not that it matters much. It's just as water-scarce as Sonora."

Yuma Bustout

All three weary riders had dismounted to spell their horses. The Rio Grande was perhaps three hours behind them now. Luckily the horses had a chance to tank up good before they rode out, for so far there had been no sign of water.

Bill studied his map, turning his back to the grit-laden wind that tore at it.

"Wish I had some bourbon, damnit," he complained.

"I had the last of it, remember?" Connie said, mustering a weak smile. "Make a note of that, Joshua. Bill's first action was to try taking advantage of an innocent girl by getting her drunk."

Bill looked up from his map. "Tell you what, Juliet. If I tried to do that, you'd know it."

Boldly she met his challenging eyes. "Well, now, I'm sure I would."

This was too much for Josh. "Where's the nearest water?" he demanded. Bill grinned at the kid before looking at his map again.

"First river we're likely to reach," he said, "is the Nueces. There's plenty of water after that. But I don't mean to take it that far."

Bill squatted and pointed to a spot in the sand. What appeared to be tacky, rust-colored mud, he explained, was in fact dried blood.

"Danford copped it bad," Bill added. "He's bleeding like a stuck pig. So the best plan is just to run those bastards down. We stay on them like ugly on a buzzard."

"Good," Connie chimed in, though she was clearly exhausted. When Josh later recorded these events, he compared her glazed, shocked eyes to those of battle veternas in Civil War photographs.

Connie added, "The harder we pursue, the less time they have . . ."

She trailed off, then said simply, "The better it will be for Anne. I just want to get this over."

God yes, Josh thought as they all swung up into leather again and prepared to ride on. *Get it over indeed*. If he never saw another damn desert in his life, that was peachy by him.

But "getting this over" was perhaps going to be even more complicated than Josh knew. Just before he spurred his roan forward, Wild Bill spent a full thirty seconds studying the creosote hills surrounding them.

"S'matter?" Josh demanded.

Bill took his time answering,

"Twice now," he said, "I've spotted glints that look just like reflecting glass."

"Could be quartz or mica," Josh suggested. "Lots of these rocks have reflecting mineral traces."

"That's right," Bill agreed. "I taught you that myself, kid, didn't I? But I still think somebody's following us."

"You mean . . . Danford or Coyote has doubled back for an ambush?"

Bill shook his head. "No, that's low odds. Danford can't do that—he's hit bad. And Coyote won't do it while Danford's alive."

"Why not?"

But it was Connie who called up the answer to that one. "Coyote is not about to leave that silver *or* Anne alone with Danford while he's still alive. Believe me, I had to look into those eyes of his."

Josh felt like Bill and Connie were picking on him. He took it out on Bill.

Yuma Bustout

"Back in Denver you said you don't get hunches, only journalists do. All this sounds like a hunch to me."

Bill ignored him for a minute, twisting around to glance at Connie. She was back in the saddle, ready when they were, and gave him a brave smile. Then Bill turned back to Josh.

"Back in Denver I lied, okay? Now you won your point, do your job. Take up the drag. You're a good writer, kid. But this ain't no time to be composing in your head. Call it a hunch, call it a full house, I don't care. Just shut up and keep an eye out. Somebody else is in the mix now, somebody who's waiting for us to get careless."

"Coyote, it's surefire, I'm telling you," Fargo Danford ranted, his words tumbling over each other in his fever delirium. "We're both plenty rich now, and I ain't talking just silver."

Anne despised Danford, but she couldn't help a little twinge of pity at his horrible plight. The man was on the threshold of death, but there he lay, scheming fortunes. How could he *not* know he was doomed? Unless, she suddenly hoped, he was denying it because he knew he was hell-bound?

"No more river-water soup for us, pard! We're rich, plenty rich!"

"Ahuh," Coyote agreed automatically, paying little attention. Anne watched him cross to a clutch of rocks and scramble to the top. When he made it, he stayed up there a long time studying every direction.

Anne could see that something had caught his eye, something that troubled him. Hope sparked within her.

"Mister, I'll warrant right now," Danford rattled on, lying on his uninjured side in the hot sand, "that fine-haired bitch is worth a fifty-thousand-dollar ransom. Add that to the silver, Coyote, huh? You know that? Add 'em up, boy! We're rich men!"

"Ahuh," Coyote called down, looking around to wink at Anne. "Maybe you could even have the Texas Rangers deliver that money, huh? They're a friendly bunch who coddle criminals."

Danford was too far gone to catch the scorn in his friend's words. "Hanh? What's that? Sure, sure, let the Rangers do it. We're rich, buddy. First thing I'm gonna do? Light up a cee-gar with a hunnert-dollar bill, hanh? That Yuma hellhole is behind us, Coyote, yessir!"

Danford coughed. Then Anne heard him swear to himself.

"Hey!" he cried out, his tone one of surprise. "Hey, look at this bleedin', Coyote. Aww, man, my shirt is soaked! Coyote! You got to stop the blood, hanh?"

"You want me to fix it?" Coyote called down.

"Sure, sure, Jesus! Fix it, Coyote! Aww, damn, it's just a-pumpin' out!"

Anne watched Coyote climb slowly down, his face an empty page. She felt dread heavy in her stomach. He confirmed her premonition when he slid the pistol from his flap holster.

But after counting the loads, Coyote holstered the pistol and picked up one of the sawed-off shotguns instead.

Danford, lying down and panting hard now, noticed none of this. "Fix it, Coyote, wouldja, huh? Jesus, fix it, please!"

Yuma Bustout

"Sure," Coyote said quietly, moving in closer to Danford where he lay in the shade of a Joshua tree. "This'll sting just a little."

Anne felt faint and turned her head away.

"Rich men," Danford muttered. "We'll be—"

Even though she knew it was coming, the explosion of the sawed-off made Anne flinch and cry out.

Anne refused to look at the body.

"Out here," she heard Coyote say behind her, "a man pulls his freight or he's a drag on the rest."

"Women too, of course?"

"Especially women," Coyote assured her.

"His plan to ransom me," Anne said.

"What about it?"

"You have no plan to return me to my husband, do you?"

When there was no response, Anne finally turned to look at him, though she refused to let her eyes focus on the dead body.

Coyote's lipless grin sent a feather tickling down her spine.

"You're as smart as you are pretty, you know that?" he goaded her. "I plan to do all the things I been thinking about doing to you for these past few days. And then, when I do 'em, I mean to kill you."

For a moment the fear left Anne, replaced by a surge of anger. This despicable pig didn't deserve the satisfaction of scaring her.

"Then why not get it over with now?" she challenged him. "Rut on me like the filthy animal you are, then kill me!"

He pointed one thumb over his shoulder. "Usual reason, sweet britches. Your sister's new stag is close on our trail. Now, get on your damn horse and ride."

"What if I refuse?" she shouted at him. "You're going to kill me anyway! Why should I do your bidding any longer?"

Coyote brought the shotgun up to the ready. Anne felt her calves go weak.

"That your final word?" he said in his atonal voice.

Anne wanted to say yes, just do it. But when she stared at those twin barrels, they stared back. And they unnerved her. Which meant she wasn't ready yet to quit fighting for her life.

Wild Bill is still coming, she reminded herself. As she struggled up onto her horse, Anne clung to that thought like a drowning man to a log. Something had troubled Coyote when he took his long look. Please let it be Hickok.

Then she noticed something. The knife protruding from Danford's boot. When Coyote bent to search the body, he forgot about it.

Coyote's back was to her now as he went to retrieve his horse.

Anne debated it for a fraction of a second, knowing he might well kill her if he caught her. But if she could just get it and hide it in her clothing before Coyote turned around . . .

True, Wild Bill was doing his level best. But what if that wasn't good enough? Didn't she have some obligation to fight her own battle? Anne reminded herself that God made Beowulf stand on his own two feet before He agreed to help him slay the dragon.

Anne let herself slide to the ground again. She moved forward quickly, praying that Coyote would not turn around before she could get it.

Chapter Sixteen

"Only one left now," Wild Bill said, still kneeling beside Danford's corpse.

Bluebottle flies covered it like a rippling cape. But carrion birds had not yet begun to gather in any numbers. Bill guessed they were only two hours, tops, behind Coyote and Anne.

"But that's assuming he's still ahead," Bill qualified. "Now he's plugged Danford, he can leave Anne tied up with the silver while he doubles back to dry-gulch us."

Bill stood and raised one arm to indicate the rolling sand hills and deep ravines surrounding them.

"Coyote's part Yaqui, and I don't know much about the tribe except they're no bunch to fool with. They're one Mexican tribe the Spanish couldn't conquer. This ain't the best ambush country, but Coyote knows how to use terrain for all it's got."

Day or night didn't determine the shifts now. Though there was still some threat from Comanches and Kiowas in this part of south Texas, it was far tamer than in the wide-open fifties and sixties. Hickok felt it was safe to show in daylight north of the border.

Wild Bill wouldn't admit it, but Josh knew—Bill was calling rests based on discreet glances at Connie to see how she was holding up. As Josh and Connie showed increasing signs of exhaustion, Hickok seemed to rejuvenate as compensation.

He stood all watches now. Amazed, Josh recorded in his notes that Wild Bill hadn't slept now—or complained about it—in over thirty hours. Josh and Connie would fall asleep almost immediately. When they woke, Bill had hot game on the spit, even if only a bit of gamy pheasant.

"Eat, children," he joked once, "you'll need your strength for school."

Josh had noticed this before about Wild Bill. He was the first man to carp when his new suit got stained or he ran out of cheroots or Old Taylor. And it downright embarrassed Josh, the way Bill would primp in front of a mirror just like a vain woman!

But when conditions truly deteriorated, when men were losing their belief in survival, Hickok rose up as a natural leader. No inspiring speeches about God, duty, and country; just grim good humor and a straight-ahead determination to keep up the strut till the job was done.

They passed a giant dry lake that Bill said marked the Dimmit County line. So far Coyote was fulfilling

Yuma Bustout

Bill's projected route—due east toward the Nueces River. Hickok still believed the half-breed meant to exchange the silver for banknotes in New Orleans.

By late morning, they were a good twenty miles past the Dimmit County line. The sand hills occasionally formed tall headlands with plenty of good hiding places above the trail. At such points, Bill usually found an alternate route even if they lost a little time.

But sometimes he couldn't. Like now, Josh told himself, noticing that the three of them were riding into a dangerous stretch. Giant rock formations, detritus from some massive geological upheaval eons ago, formed impassable terrain on both sides of the narrow sand wash that served as trail.

Hickok, riding point, raised an arm to halt them. Josh rode up from the drag to join him and Connie.

"We can't circle wide," Bill told his companions, "without losing too much time."

He looked again at the dangerous stretch, then at Connie.

"Please don't send me back with Josh," she pleaded with Hickok. "I know there's danger, and I know you're responsible for me. But you yourself said Josh is a good man to have along. Please, Bill? We're so close to saving Anne, I can just feel it in my heart! I want to be there when we rescue her. Please?"

Bill grinned and shook his head. "Why should *I* be the first man who can resist you? All right."

Connie grinned back. But Bill's smile faded fast.

"Listen, you two. Coyote doesn't care about killing you—it's me he's got to fret, and he knows it. That's a damned shooting gallery we're about to ride through, with us the moving targets. If Coyote drops me, Longfellow, you've got one assignment. Let me hear it."

"Get Connie back to Arizona," Josh replied.

Bill nodded. "At the first telegraph office you reach, you contact Pinkerton in Denver and give him all you know. He'll take it from there."

"In that case, what about Anne?" Connie protested.

Bill didn't baby her. "If Coyote kills me," he told her bluntly, "Anne's as good as dead too. Believe me, you and Josh won't stop him. The kid has his orders, and he'll follow them, because he's a good trooper."

"Hear that?" Connie told Josh. "Even riding into possible death, you're still 'the kid.' I wonder if Wild Bill Hickok ever kissed his mother?"

Bill scowled. One thing he hated, Josh knew from experience, was when folks pushed too far into his personal life.

"Hickok has kissed plenty of women," Bill assured her. "And when I kiss them, they *stay* kissed. I've also taken a few over my knee, too, and warmed up their backsides good for them, taught them a little respect for their elders."

She flushed and started to retort. But Bill cut her off.

"This ain't another dress rehearsal, sweetheart. Save it for the stage, we've got to move out. Joshua!" he added, emphasizing the name for her benefit. "I want you to ride closer to Miss Pink Cheeks. If Coyote jumps us, make sure you get her covered down."

For the next hour they rode on unmolested. Despite Bill's conviction that trouble awaited them in the rock formations, Josh had almost concluded Hickok's trail instincts were wrong this time.

Yuma Bustout

Still, it was one of the eeriest stretches Josh had ever ridden since coming west. The ground beneath the horses' hooves was mostly hardpan that threw off clopping echoes from the surrounding rock walls.

There was no sign of life—human, animal, or plant. Just the smooth pan of the narrowing wash, with sand drifting across it, and the massive, striated rock rising around them to heights of more than several hundred feet.

Then, abruptly, they rode through the last dogleg turn, and there it was: clear blue sky out ahead where the rock formations dwindled off to low sand hills again.

Home free, Josh told himself with a fluming sigh of relief. And halfway into that sigh, a rifle spoke its deadly piece from above them, shattering the tomblike quiet.

That first bullet impacted only inches from Fireaway's front hooves, and the roan reared up, nickering. But Wild Bill didn't fight his horse when it began crow-hopping—the animal was bullet-trained and now made Coyote earn his target.

Again, again, the carbine cracked with a shattering racket in that closed-in defile. The bullets, ricocheting from stone surface to stone surface, sent off a screaming whine that especially agitated the horses.

Nonetheless, Josh remembered his orders. He managed to seize the bridle of Connie's horse and get it turned around with his.

Josh spurred his buckskin down their back trail, back through the safety of the bend. Bill's orders had been to flee back toward Arizona *if* Hickok was killed. But last Josh saw of him, Wild Bill was still alive. So Josh reined in at the first good hiding place, a cleft in the rock wall made by water erosion.

"In there!" he ordered Connie. Josh whapped her horse on the rump hard, moving it into the narrow enclosure.

Josh heard more rifle shots, then the distinctive sound of Bill's Peacemakers. But Hickok evidently hit nothing, because Josh could hear him racing back along the trail.

"This spot will do," he said when he joined them. "For Connie. Kid, are you willing to provide me some cover? It won't put you in the line of fire—exactly."

Bill slid his Winchester from the boot and held it out. Josh took it. Bill also reached into a saddle bag, then handed Josh a box of shells.

"We'll put you just partway into the bend," Bill said. "So you can toss a shot up there now and then. Just aim for the rimrock, then adjust if you see his muzzle smoke. Which I doubt you will, knowing Coyote. I just want you to keep him interested so he stays where he's at."

"Where will you be?" Connie demanded.

"I think I can find a way through the rocks to the back, sneak up on him from behind him."

Connie paled. "Sneak up on Coyote? Is that smart?"

Bill snorted, shaking his head while he hobbled his horse with the other two.

"Smart? Juliet, sneaking up on Coyote is about as stupid as a man can get. Downright suicidal, matter of fact."

Yuma Bustout

"Then why are you doing it?" she demanded.

Bill was already heading back through the bend, Josh on his heels carrying the Winchester.

"Because I'm out of cigars," he said with dead seriousness. "And the sooner I kill Coyote, the quicker I light up."

Wild Bill couldn't swear this was the hardest climb he'd ever made. But he was damned if it didn't rate high among the worst.

First he had positioned Josh behind an abutment of hard granite, maybe halfway into the bend. Bill hoped he was right in his calculation that Coyote couldn't spot muzzle flash at his angle from above.

Now Josh was dutifully firing a round up topside every minute or so. And as Bill had calculated, the half-breed was returning an occasional shot based on ear-targeting. Coyote was hoping for a ricochet, for in that virtual world of stone below, each shot became many, many more before the bullet fragmented.

Josh was relatively safe from those ricochets, Bill figured, if the kid had enough horse sense to stay covered. Not so for Bill himself. Although Coyote couldn't see him, Bill had to stay exposed while he desperately searched for some opening through the jumble of rocks.

Coyote fired, and a bullet whanged off rock, began its piercing whine as it bounced from surface to surface. Another, and this time Bill started when the slug threw rock dust in his face.

During all this Wild Bill scrambled among the rocks like a nervous monkey, seeking some opening.

He spotted a place where two odd-shaped rocks left a small hole between them.

Bill had no idea if it would lead all the way through. But nothing better showed itself, and bullets were nipping at his sitter. Tossing his hat down, Bill wriggled into the opening.

The passage was narrow to begin with and got even tighter as Hickok progressed inch by inch on bleeding, scraped elbows and knees. At one point Bill had to fight down a welling sense of "cooped-in" panic—he was wedged tight, unable to go forward, unable to retreat.

Bill willed himself calm. Then he relaxed his muscles and expelled all the air in his chest. This left him just barely enough room to squeeze forward again—and up ahead, Bill saw blessed light.

But as he pushed through and looked upward, he realized he had a hard climb ahead of him.

But there! There was Anne, huddled up in the rimrock. And though Hickok could spot only the back of Coyote's gray flannel shirt, he saw that Anne was tied to his belt by a lead line around her waist.

At first Bill found some helpful hand-and footholds. But these thinned out as he gained altitude. At times he was forced to haul himself up hand over hand, with virtually no footholds.

By the time Anne spotted Bill, his arms were trembling violently. So violently, he feared he might drop at any moment.

Bill winked to calm Anne, who he feared might give him away. As he strained to inch himself up to a little ledge behind her, he could hear good old Josh plinking away, keeping Coyote's attention.

Yuma Bustout

Now Bill was only inches from gaining the security of the ledge. But his tortured arms felt stretched to the point of tearing.

Bill closed his eyes and pictured a morning nine years earlier in the beautiful Shenendoah Valley. He had spied on Stonewall Jackson motivating his troops for a battle: *Gentlemen, today you must exert yourselves!*

Hickok gave it his best effort and gained the ledge behind Anne Jacobs. Two seconds after he was safe, the ledge collapsed under him.

God kiss me, Hickok thought even as he made a wild stab at the more solid rim that held Connie and the half-breed. His left arm snagged it, and Wild Bill hung at a precarious angle.

As rocks and gravel tumbled and slid down, Coyote whirled and discovered his enemy only a few feet away. For once those bone-button eyes registered some emotion, though Bill had no luxury to read it.

Then, emitting a little cry of triumph, Coyote quickly jacked a round into the chamber of the Spencer carbine.

Because he had needed both hands to climb, both of Bill's Colts were still holstered. Despite his wildly dramatic enactments with Buffalo Bill Cody's Wild West Show, this gun battle now was unprecedented in Hickok's memory.

Coyote brought his muzzle down to fire. Bill, dangling by one arm, legs flailing, still managed to somehow speed-draw and plug Coyote.

The impact knocked Coyote backward. But Bill cussed when he realized it had not been a fatal hit.

153

Judd Cole

Coyote, blood pumping from his right thigh, stepped sideways, and Bill had no line of fire from his restricted position.

Nor could he establish a better one, for he had absolutely no footholds—the slide had taken all of them with it. All he could do was hang here by one already exhausted arm, waiting to either get shot or fall to his death on the rocks below.

Coyote leaned out, grinned his lipless grin, and lowered his gun muzzle until it kissed a spot just behind Bill's right ear.

"Say good-bye to your soul, Wild Bill," Coyote called down. "The hole you put in me can be patched up."

With a piercing scream to focus her strength and will, Anne pulled the knife from her bodice and drove it hard into Coyote's back.

"You goddamned bitch!" Coyote snarled, blood bubbling from his lips. But his legs suddenly folded like empty sacks.

"Don't let him fall!" Bill warned her. Not only would the falling body take Hickok with it, but Anne was still tied to her captor. All three of them would die.

With Bill shoving up from below and Anne tugging from above, they kept Coyote from dropping.

Bill was on his last reserve of strength. "Anne! Untie that rope from your arm and throw it down here. Leave it tied to Coyote! Then I want you to pile some rocks on his body, hear me? Hurry, Anne, I can't hang on much longer!"

Anne scrambled to save her hero. When she had the body sufficiently weighted down to hold him, Bill pulled himself up.

Yuma Bustout

"Permission to kiss a married woman," Bill said, greeting the governor's wife.

"Permission granted," she assured Hickok, crystal dollops of tears welling from her eyes as she stepped into Bill's arms.

Chapter Seventeen

The one-horse burg called Hondo, Texas, was located about forty miles west of San Antonio. It was a sleepy, insignificant crossroads hamlet where little disturbed the dusty twang of grasshopper wings. Nobody ever came *to* Hondo—they just occasionally passed through on their way someplace else.

Located one mile west of town was a huge earthquake fissure known as Thompson's Chasm. Miles long and more than thirty feet wide, it plunged deeper than anyone had ever measured. Because the only good road in that neck of south Texas was bisected by the chasm, a narrow rope-suspension bridge had been built to cross it.

However, the bridge had been no great engineering feat even when it was new twenty years earlier. By now dry rot and termites had made it flimsy, if not quite unreliable.

Replacing it would have required more funds than the residents of Hondo—population seventeen—could earn by passing the hat. In lieu of replacement, one civic-minded local had scrawled two hand-lettered signs on boards and nailed one at each end of the thirty-foot bridge:

CAWSHUN, RYDERS!!! ONLEY
ONE HORSS AT A TYME ON
THIS BRIJ! LEED YER HORSS!

Butch Jeffries had carefully ascertained that Hickok's party would be riding this way. And because he had killed successfully at Thompson's Chasm before, Butch chose it as the best place to kill Connie Emmerick.

From where he stood now, atop a redrock butte a few hundred feet north of the bridge, it was a clear shot at a sharp downward angle. As he knew from experience, a rider was virtually helpless once gunfire erupted.

Not only would the bridge support only one horse and rider, it swayed and bounced dangerously if even that one horse tried to move too quickly. Which meant Butch would not be limited to one shot at Connie—and nobody could help her without collapsing that bridge.

As for any pursuit afterward, that was hindered. Sure, the rock-strewn grade between this butte and the road could be climbed. But it was a slow uphill climb, perhaps a forty-five-degree slope—and meantime, Butch would be opening up a good lead on a fresh horse. And nobody knew this country like he did.

Yuma Bustout

No tangles with Hickok, thank you. Just a "shoot and scoot," as Butch called such jobs.

Jeffries removed a Volcanic Arms repeating rifle from its buckskin sheath. He opened the loading gate and then took a handful of copper-jacketed slugs from a chamois pouch on his belt, thumbing them into the weapon through a well above the trigger guard.

Twelve shots loaded into the spring-feed mechanism. But Butch didn't plan to take that many shots, not with Hickok down there.

It wouldn't matter. On that rickety bridge, a miss was as good as a hit. If Emmerick's horse shied even a little, the swaying bridge would pitch her into that hungry maw below.

Suddenly, Butch remembered she was an actress.

"Break a leg, Miss Emmerick," he said out loud, jacking a round into the chamber.

"The silver belongs to the Denver Mint," Bill explained. "But there'll be the standard recovery fee of a thousand dollars. That's still better than a poke in the eye with a sharp stick."

"Man alive! You bet it is," Josh agreed, doing some quick arithmetic in his head. "You'd have to give Pinkerton two hundred full days work for that kind of money."

"Only a hundred days," Bill corrected him. "Half that recovery fee is yours, kid. You earned it, fair and square."

"Mine?"

"So send it to your ma if you don't want it. You earned it. You been here beside me eating dust and ducking bullets every mile of the way."

"I have, haven't I?" Josh agreed. "Heck, I'll take it. It's just—I ain't never had five hundred dollars."

Bill winked. "First time I get you near a deck of cards, you *won't* have it."

"Bill Hickok!" Connie scolded. "He's still an innocent lad despite your influence! Joshua, *do* send your share to your mother. I do believe Bill would rob a poor box to finance his vices."

Bill tipped his hat to her. "I've done that," he confessed, deadpan. "I'm in Satan's grip, no question."

The four of them—Wild Bill, Josh, Connie, and Anne—were on their way to the train station in San Antonio. That was far preferable to a long, hot horseback ride back to Yuma. Especially hauling a cache of silver bars.

For everyone except Wild Bill, this ride had become an almost festive occasion. Hickok, however, refused to relax his hair-trigger alertness. And Josh knew why. Bill still believed, based on those distant glints he'd spotted the day before, that a second source of danger plagued them.

So far today, Bill had spotted nothing worrisome. But that changed when the bridge over Thompson's Chasm finally eased into view.

He halted them, making everyone cover behind their horses. Bill read the sign. Then he studied the surrounding terrain carefully before studying his map.

Wild Bill shook his head. "Looks too much like a stacked deck to me. But by my map, it's thirty miles or better of hard riding before that damned chasm gets small enough to cross. No more roads or bridges hereabouts."

Bill ignored everyone for the next few minutes,

Yuma Bustout

swinging down from his horse. Josh watched him boldly stand out in the open. He dropped down on one knee, squinting and looking toward that distant redrock butte above them on the rock slope.

"He calls that 'following the bullet back to the gun,'" Josh explained quietly to the two fascinated women. "I've seen him do it before. He figures the best place for a marksman to be, then guesses the bullet trajectory."

"In other words, you're saying he takes the role of the killer," Connie suggested. "And look at that enjoyment on his face. He does it well."

"He's a born killer himself," Josh conceded. "But I've never seen him kill anyone who didn't require killing."

Bill stood up and looped the roan's reins around his wrist.

"I'm going over first with my horse," he announced. "Then one at a time I take the pack animals. After I'm done, Anne comes. Then Connie, then Josh. Anne, wait until I get into a good firing position on the other side before you come over."

Josh fought down nervous stirrings in his stomach as Hickok led Fire-away across without incident. Then Bill led both of the silver-laden pack animals across and hobbled them.

Bill took up a secure position, his Winchester resting on a rock so it had a good line of fire to that redrock butte above them.

Josh felt his muscles relaxing as the threat obviously diminished. Hickok was the only target worth shooting at.

Nonetheless, Bill played it cautious.

"Go ahead, Anne!" he called over.

Although the swaying bridge clearly made her nervous, the governor's resolute wife crossed without incident.

"Cue call for Juliet!" Hickok sang out, clearly in a lighter mood now himself. "Or shall I carry you across?"

Connie shook a fist at him. "Wouldn't you love that?"

"Damn straight!" Hickok, who had been checking the sight line down his barrel, looked across at her and grinned wide. "I promise to hold on tight."

Connie eased out onto the bridge, leading her blood bay. She paused when the bridge began to sway a little.

"It's all right, hon," Anne called out. "You're doing fine."

By now Hickok had no idea about Connie's progress, for he was engrossed in studying that butte. He had little expectation of trouble now, but the old habit of caution kept him alert.

Had the hidden rifleman blued his barrel, Bill would never have seen him in time. But exposed metal caught just enough sun to glint.

Bill's battle-trained reflexes didn't wait for further confirmation of trouble. Using that glint as a reference point, Hickok methodically and rapidly emptied the Winchester, holding a tight pattern with the glint at its core.

Anne screamed, and Connie's horse began backing up as Bill opened fire. But Bill quit firing almost immediately, and the bay settled down.

Josh felt his jaw drop open in astonishment when, all of a moment, a man came plunging down that steep slope above them. He was only wounded, and

Yuma Bustout

still alive, for Josh could hear him screaming as he slammed from rock to rock, plummeting downward toward the shocked travelers. His rifle clattered along behind him like a faithful pet.

Though his only gunshot wound was to the knee, the battering tumble killed the sniper before he quit rolling, stopping only about twenty yards away from the far end of the bridge.

Wild Bill coaxed a shaken Connie across. Then he crossed quickly to join Joshua at the body.

Bill rolled it over with one foot.

"Butch Jeffries," he announce after some study. "I played poker with him once—El Paso I think it was. That was before he got a reputation as a hired gun."

"But why Connie?" Josh demanded. "I can see wanting to kidnap and ransom her, but what's the profit in killing her?"

The answer to that question turned up when Wild Bill searched the body and found a little leather-bound diary in the chamois pouch on his belt.

Perhaps for purposes of blackmail, or simply because he was a man to keep accounts, that diary showed fifteen years' worth of careful entries: dates, amounts paid by whom and for what purposes.

Wild Bill's mustache was still badly singed from the explosion beside the Rio Grande. Now Josh watched him thoughtfully finger the burnt stubble while he read the most recent entry.

"Well, God kiss me," Bill said with quiet disbelief. He looked across the bridge toward Connie, then handed the diary to Josh. "Answer your question, kid?"

Josh read the entry for June 12, 1872: *$5,000 from Jim Paxton to kill his fiancée. Proud bastard says he* *can't abide spoiled goods. Figures if the convicts don't poke her, Hickok will.*

Josh swallowed, waiting for his anger and disbelief to subside.

"You showing this to her?" he asked Bill.

"Hell, kid. Doesn't she have the right to know why her fiancée is going to prison? This is going straight to the circuit judge in Yuma. Paxton's kind gets away with murder plenty. But he fouled his nest when he tried to put the quietus on America's Sweetheart. Nobody will dare to cover him."

"I'll make sure of that," Josh vowed. "I'll put that scoundrel's name out over the wires. The newspapers will hang him first."

Bill nodded, standing back up to cross the bridge with this troubling news. "Good. I'm not too fond of the crapsheets. But sometimes we need a public hanging."

Jim Paxton was indeed publicly "hanged" in the newspapers. The courts, too, exacted their punishment in a fitting twist of fate: Convicted of a murder-for-hire scheme, the cattleman was sentenced to ten years at hard labor and confined in the Territorial Prison at Yuma.

As for Connie Emmerick, neither Wild Bill nor Josh was unduly surprised when the news of Paxton's treachery made her withdraw inside herself. She promptly returned to Boston, and both men figured they'd never see her again.

As for Hickok, he was bound and determined to finally have the big time that Pinkerton kept spoiling. He and Josh took rooms once again at the Crystal Palace Hotel in Denver.

Yuma Bustout

After some careful diplomacy, Wild Bill managed to smooth the ruffled feathers of Marie Marchand—the French coquette who sang at the city's most popular music hall. Bill convinced her that only urgent duties had forced him to stand her up last time.

As Wild Bill, with the lovely Marie on his arm, strolled into the leather-plush lobby of the Crystal Palace, Josh hurried to intercept him.

"Bill! Glad I caught you. You can't—"

Hickok, sleek and debonair in a new summer-weight suit, raised a hand to silence his friend.

"Longfellow, I don't care what it is. The lady and I will not be interrupted under any circumstances."

"No, Bill, you don't understand. You can't—"

"Kid, *you* don't understand. I don't care if it's Pinkerton or Queen Victoria, *nobody* interrupts me this evening. I just gave you five hundred dollars today—go paint the town, why'n't you?"

Josh surrendered with a shrug. "All right. Just remember, I tried to warn you."

A bottle of Old Taylor in his left hand, Marie on his right, Bill headed up to his top-floor suite. He keyed the lock, swept open the door, and invited Marie in first. He stepped in behind her, then pulled up short, staring at the wing chair beside the highboy.

Connie Emmerick, looking lovely in a wine-colored dress trimmed with velvet and dyed feathers, sat waiting in the chair.

Marie stared at the lovely actress; Connie stared at the pretty singer. Bill just stood there, looking like a man who had been hit hard but not quite dropped.

"Connie," Bill said, mustering a nervy little smile. "You might have mentioned you were coming."

"I wanted to surprise you, and evidently I did. You

165

see, *Mister* Hickok, I began to think about it. So many people were speculating about us, about whether we . . . well, at any rate. It occurred to me that despite all the speculation, you were a perfect gentleman. I began to feel insecure about that. So I came back out west to find out if you *are* just a gentleman or whether you simply are not interested."

Josh appeared in the doorway just in time to see Connie rise and gather up her purse.

"Oh, I'm definitely interested," Bill hastened to inform Connie. But this was another mistake. Marie slapped him so hard, she left an imprint of her hand on his cheek.

"Monsieur Hickok," she informed him with chilly dignity before she flounced out of the room. "Perhaps the women *you* require live in wooden cribs on Railroad Street?"

Connie, too, archly walked past Bill. She took Josh by the arm. "Joshua?" she said sweetly, "would you be willing to escort a single lady around town?"

Alone in his room, Bill cursed until he'd used up every swearword he knew.

"At least I'll get drunk in peace, goddamnit," he told his reflection in the mirror.

But even as Bill poured his first pony glass full of bourbon, a figure appeared in the open doorway. A stout, homely young woman with her greasy hair tied in a knot under her immaculate gray Stetson. She wore men's clothing, a .44 sagging down her right thigh.

And clearly, judging by the way she wobbled on her feet, Calamity Jane was drunker than the lords of Creation.

"God dawg!" she exclaimed in her gravel-pan voice.

Yuma Bustout

"Bill Hickok, you purty son of trouble, I been in jail so long I'm horny as a brass band! I'm comin' to climb all over you, darlin'!"

Jane stumbled into the room and closed the door with her heel, never taking her eyes off the handsome man trapped within, panic in his eyes.

MAX BRAND
THE WORLD'S MOST CELEBRATED WESTERN WRITER!

Ronicky Doone. From Tombstone to Sonora, Ronicky Doone has won the respect of every law-abiding citizen—and the hatred of every bushwhacking bandit. But Bill Gregg isn't one to let a living legend get in his way. What nobody tells Gregg is that Doone doesn't enjoy living his hard-riding, rip-roaring life unless he takes a chance on losing it once in a while.
_3738-6 $3.99 US/$4.99 CAN

Ronicky Doone's Treasure. Hunting down a fortune in hidden loot, Jack Moon and his wild bunch swear to string up or shoot down anyone who stands in their way. Then Ronicky Doone crosses their path, and he'll need a shootist's skill and a gambler's luck to survive. If that isn't enough, his only reward will be a pine box.
_3748-3 $3.99 US/$4.99 CAN

Ronicky Doone's Reward. No stranger to trouble, Doone isn't surprised to find himself in the midst of a deadly war between two rival families. The odds are ten to one that Doone will wind up on Boot Hill—and even money that anyone drawing against him will eat hot lead.
_3779-3 $3.99 US/$4.99 CAN

Dorchester Publishing Co., Inc.
P.O. Box 6640
Wayne, PA 19087-8640

Please add $1.75 for shipping and handling for the first book and $.50 for each book thereafter. NY, NYC, and PA residents, please add appropriate sales tax. No cash, stamps, or C.O.D.s. All orders shipped within 6 weeks via postal service book rate. Canadian orders require $2.00 extra postage and must be paid in U.S. dollars through a U.S. banking facility.

Name_____
Address_____
City_____ State_____ Zip_____
I have enclosed $_____ in payment for the checked book(s).
Payment <u>must</u> accompany all orders. ❏ Please send a free catalog.

A BALLAD FOR SALLIE
JUDY ALTER

Longhair Jim Courtright has been both a marshal and a desperado—and in Hell's Half Acre, the roughest part of Fort Worth, he is a living legend. His skill with a gun has made him a hero in some people's eyes . . . and a killer in others'. As soon as young widow Sallie McNutt steps off the stage from Tennessee, her refined manners and proper attire set her apart from the other women of the Half Acre. And it isn't long before something else sets her apart—someone wants her dead.

___4365-3 $4.50 US/$5.50 CAN

Dorchester Publishing Co., Inc.
P.O. Box 6640
Wayne, PA 19087-8640

Please add $1.75 for shipping and handling for the first book and $.50 for each book thereafter. NY, NYC, and PA residents, please add appropriate sales tax. No cash, stamps, or C.O.D.s. All orders shipped within 6 weeks via postal service book rate. Canadian orders require $2.00 extra postage and must be paid in U.S. dollars through a U.S. banking facility.

Name_____
Address_____
City_____State_____Zip_____
I have enclosed $_____in payment for the checked book(s).
Payment <u>must</u> accompany all orders. ❑ Please send a free catalog.

MAX BRAND
THE ABANDONED OUTLAW

No writer captures the American West better than Max Brand. And nowhere is Brand's talent more evident than in these three classic short novels, all restored to their original length, and collected in paperback for the first time. In "The Gold King Turns His Back," young Miriam Standard is more than capable of running her father's ranch, but finds she has much to learn about the Westerners' meaning of honor. In "The Three Crosses," an ominous prediction leads a cowpuncher to a showdown with a notorious gunfighter. And the title novel finds a young woman caught in the middle of a lifelong rivalry between two men, one of whom is an outlaw. Experience the West as only Max Brand could write it!

___4465-X $4.50 US/$5.50 CAN

Dorchester Publishing Co., Inc.
P.O. Box 6640
Wayne, PA 19087-8640

Please add $1.75 for shipping and handling for the first book and $.50 for each book thereafter. NY, NYC, and PA residents, please add appropriate sales tax. No cash, stamps, or C.O.D.s. All orders shipped within 6 weeks via postal service book rate. Canadian orders require $2.00 extra postage and must be paid in U.S. dollars through a U.S. banking facility.

Name_____
Address_____
City_____ State _____ Zip _____
I have enclosed $_____ in payment for the checked book(s).
Payment <u>must</u> accompany all orders. ☐ Please send a free catalog.

WILL CADE
Larimont

John Kendall doesn't want to go back home to Larimont, Montana. He has to—to investigate the death of his father. At first everyone believed that Bill Kendall died in a tragic fire... until an autopsy reveals a bullet hole in Bill's head. But why is the local marshal keeping it a secret? John isn't quite sure, so he sets out to find the truth for himself. But the more he looks into his father's death, the more secrets he uncovers—and the more resistance he meets. It seems there are a whole lot of folks who don't want John nosing around, folks with a whole lot to lose if the truth comes out. But John won't stop until he digs up the last secret. Even if it is one better left buried.

___4618-0 $4.50 US/$5.50 CAN

Dorchester Publishing Co., Inc.
P.O. Box 6640
Wayne, PA 19087-8640

Please add $1.75 for shipping and handling for the first book and $.50 for each book thereafter. NY, NYC, and PA residents, please add appropriate sales tax. No cash, stamps, or C.O.D.s. All orders shipped within 6 weeks via postal service book rate. Canadian orders require $2.00 extra postage and must be paid in U.S. dollars through a U.S. banking facility.

Name_____
Address_____
City_____State_____Zip_____
I have enclosed $_____ in payment for the checked book(s).
Payment <u>must</u> accompany all orders. ❏ Please send a free catalog.
CHECK OUT OUR WEBSITE! www.dorchesterpub.com

MOVING ON
JANE CANDIA COLEMAN

Jane Candia Coleman is a magical storyteller who spins brilliant tales of human survival, hope, and courage on the American frontier, and nowhere is her marvelous talent more in evidence than in this acclaimed collection of her finest work. From a haunting story of the night Billy the Kid died, to a dramatic account of a breathtaking horse race, including two stories that won the prestigious Spur Award, here is a collection that reveals the passion and fortitude of its characters, and also the power of a wonderful writer.

___4545-1 $4.99 US/$5.99 CAN

Dorchester Publishing Co., Inc.
P.O. Box 6640
Wayne, PA 19087-8640

Please add $1.75 for shipping and handling for the first book and $.50 for each book thereafter. NY, NYC, and PA residents, please add appropriate sales tax. No cash, stamps, or C.O.D.s. All orders shipped within 6 weeks via postal service book rate. Canadian orders require $2.00 extra postage and must be paid in U.S. dollars through a U.S. banking facility.

Name_____
Address_____
City_____State_____Zip_____
I have enclosed $_____ in payment for the checked book(s).
Payment <u>must</u> accompany all orders. ❑ Please send a free catalog.
CHECK OUT OUR WEBSITE! www.dorchesterpub.com

CHEYENNE

BLOODY BONES CANYON/ RENEGADE SIEGE

JUDD COLE

Bloody Bones Canyon. Only Touch the Sky can defend them from the warriors that threaten to take over the camp. But when his people need him most, the mighty shaman is forced to avenge the slaughter of their peace chief. Even Touch the Sky cannot fight two battles at once, and without his powerful magic his people will be doomed.

And in the same action-packed volume...

Renegade Siege. Touch the Sky's blood enemies have surrounded a pioneer mining camp and are preparing to sweep down on it like a killing wind. If the mighty shaman cannot hold off the murderous attack, the settlers will be wiped out... and Touch the Sky's own camp will be next!

___4586-9 $4.99 US/$5.99 CAN

Dorchester Publishing Co., Inc.
P.O. Box 6640
Wayne, PA 19087-8640

Please add $1.75 for shipping and handling for the first book and $.50 for each book thereafter. NY, NYC, and PA residents, please add appropriate sales tax. No cash, stamps, or C.O.D.s. All orders shipped within 6 weeks via postal service book rate. Canadian orders require $2.00 extra postage and must be paid in U.S. dollars through a U.S. banking facility.

Name_____
Address_____
City_____State_____Zip_____
I have enclosed $_____ in payment for the checked book(s).
Payment <u>must</u> accompany all orders. ❏ Please send a free catalog.
CHECK OUT OUR WEBSITE! www.dorchesterpub.com

BACK TO MALACHI

ROBERT J. CONLEY
THREE-TIME SPUR AWARD-WINNER

Charlie Black is a young half-breed caught between two worlds. He is drawn to the promise of the white man's wealth, but torn by his proud heritage as a Cherokee. Charlie's pretty young fiancée yearns for the respectability of a Christian marriage and baptized children. But Charlie can't forsake his two childhood friends, Mose and Henry Pathkiller, who live in the hills with an old full-blooded Indian named Malachi. When Mose runs afoul of the law, Charlie has to choose between the ways of his fiancée and those of his friends and forefathers. He has to choose between surrender and bloodshed.

___4277-0 $3.99 US/$4.99 CAN

Dorchester Publishing Co., Inc.
P.O. Box 6640
Wayne, PA 19087-8640

Please add $1.75 for shipping and handling for the first book and $.50 for each book thereafter. NY, NYC, and PA residents, please add appropriate sales tax. No cash, stamps, or C.O.D.s. All orders shipped within 6 weeks via postal service book rate. Canadian orders require $2.00 extra postage and must be paid in U.S. dollars through a U.S. banking facility.

Name_____
Address_____
City_____State_____Zip_____
I have enclosed $_____ in payment for the checked book(s).
Payment <u>must</u> accompany all orders. ☐ Please send a free catalog.

ELIZABETH, BY NAME
WILL COOK

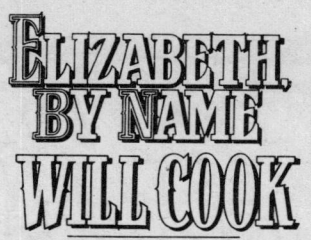

Bestselling Author Of *Sabrina Kane*

IN THE EARLY DAYS OF THE TEXAS TERRITORY, ONLY THOSE WITH COURAGE AND STRENGTH CAN SURVIVE....

There is a cattle crossing at Mustang Creek. It is miles from anywhere, and no one has ever lived there—until Elizabeth Rettig comes. Since she knows the Texans will be driving their great herds of longhorns by on the way to Dodge, she sets up a trading post.

The territory is plagued by deadly tornadoes, burning summers, and freezing winters. Indians and trail hands and vicious, lawless men ride past on their way to fame or infamy. And because Elizabeth is young and spirited, suitors come too. But only the man with the strength to tame the wild land—and the patience to outlast Elizabeth's stubbornness—will win her heart.

_3868-4 $4.99 US/$6.99 CAN

Dorchester Publishing Co., Inc.
P.O. Box 6640
Wayne, PA 19087-8640

Please add $1.75 for shipping and handling for the first book and $.50 for each book thereafter. NY, NYC, and PA residents, please add appropriate sales tax. No cash, stamps, or C.O.D.s. All orders shipped within 6 weeks via postal service book rate. Canadian orders require $2.00 extra postage and must be paid in U.S. dollars through a U.S. banking facility.

Name_____
Address_____
City_____State_____Zip_____
I have enclosed $_____ in payment for the checked book(s).
Payment <u>must</u> accompany all orders. ❏ Please send a free catalog.

ATTENTION WESTERN CUSTOMERS!

SPECIAL TOLL-FREE NUMBER
1-800-481-9191

*Call Monday through Friday
10 a.m. to 9 p.m.
Eastern Time
Get a free catalogue,
join the Western Book Club,
and order books using your
Visa, MasterCard,
or Discover®*

Leisure Books

GO ONLINE WITH US AT DORCHESTERPUB.COM